Finding Mia

Dianne J. Wilson

Finding Mia

Contact Information: titleadmin@pelicanbookgroup.com

Cover Art by *Nicola Martinez*

Harbourlight Books, a division of Pelican Ventures, LLC
www.pelicanbookgroup.com PO Box 1738 *Aztec, NM * 87410

Harbourlight Books sail and mast logo is a trademark of Pelican Ventures, LLC

Publishing History
First Harbourlight Edition, 2015
Paperback Edition ISBN 978-1-61116-445-9
Electronic Edition ISBN 978-1-61116-444-2
Published in the United States of America

Dedication

To my family, my very own 'mines', thank you for sharing me with my laptop and the people in my head.

Praise

"Finding Mia is a satisfying read with an inspiring message. Wilson has crafted a vivid cast of memorable characters and woven their lives together with just the right proportions of mystery, suspense, romance, humor, heartache and divine intervention to keep readers entertained until the final sentence. I particularly enjoyed her distinctive imagery laced throughout the story that enhances the hopeful message that there is no brokenness beyond being made whole where divine love is concerned."

~Wendy Koll

"Reading the first draft of Finding Mia, I was enchanted firstly by the style of writing which was descriptive and exciting and then the story line... I was captivated from the opening paragraph to the final page. A gripping read."

~Arlene Thomas

"I was drawn into the story from the first line, compelled and intrigued to read and read until the very last word! A person missing this book is doing themselves an injustice."

~Barbi van Rooyen

1

Isobel bit her paintbrush in frustration. The sea before her sparkled in shades of turquoise as it stretched up to kiss the rays of the sun. The beach was deserted. A slight breeze tiptoed across the tops of the waves and threaded through stately palm fronds. The entire scene screamed, *paint me.*

She put down her paintbrush, knuckling the small of her back. This place was perfect. If there were any inspiration left in the world for her, surely it would be here. But her canvas remained stubbornly blank. It mocked her in its sheer whiteness. If it were a kid, it would be sticking out its tongue and blowing raspberries.

She glared back at it for a moment. "Fine. Whatever." Ten years of this had taken its toll on her. A decade of jammed-up talent. She reached up to tie back her brown hair. It was just that—brown. Not russet or tan or chocolate. Just brown. She caught sight of a stain on her shorts. What on earth? She picked at it with her nail and ran it across her tongue. Ice cream. Isobel frowned; it was from that kid in the park. Now she was doomed to be sticky all day. There were a few reasons she wasn't keen on kids—sticky stains joined the list.

"This is all your fault, you daft canvas. If you'd

just stop sulking and let me paint something, I wouldn't have been in that park. Aaar—" Her frustrated growl was cut short by soft whimpering.

Isobel froze, listening.

Nothing.

She waited, hardly breathing.

There it was again, the faintest moan. It was coming from up the beach to the right.

Not stopping to think, she followed the sound.

Across a blinding expanse of white sand, a man-size piece of landlocked driftwood sat brooding, vulture-like. The noise came from the other side. She could hear it clearly now. It grew fainter as she got closer. Instinct kicked in. Isobel stepped out of her shoes and ran. The driftwood snagged her shorts as she climbed between two branches and she pulled hard, ripping a hole in the fabric and sending her headfirst into the sand on the other side. She spat grains out of her mouth and looked around.

There! Baking in the scorching sun, a little bundle in pink. What kind of flotsam comes in pink? She rubbed her eyes to make sure she was seeing right.

It was a child, no more than two years old, a girl with wispy blonde hair. She lay still on the burning sand, no hint that she was alive.

Time turned to treacle as Isobel rushed closer, fearing the worst.

The child was tied to the wood with a scarlet silk scarf. Isobel slipped the knot free and gingerly picked up the toddler who hung limp in her arms. Her skin was hot against Isobel's. She was a mess of tearstains and angry sunburn. "Oh, you poor baby. How long have you been out here? Where's your mum?"

Isobel scanned the beach. No one. Just a pair of

sandals midway to the water and her own farther from the water line. The little girl in her arms drew a shuddery breath, sending twin jolts of hope and fear through Isobel. No time to look for family. She needed help now.

Isobel struggled through the soft sand, though her burden was feather-light. Hers was the only car in the parking lot. She placed her charge on the back seat and drove the unfamiliar streets, fighting rising panic. An old man was waiting by a postbox for his collie to finish sniffing. She skidded to a stop.

"Excuse me. I need a doctor. Can you help?"

"Sorry, what?" He leaned in close.

Her heart sank. "A doctor! I need a doctor."

"Aaah. Turn left at the end of this road. Make your way to the t-junction and head right. Can't miss it."

Left, then right. She drove off, scared to go too fast and scared to go too slow.

Nothing. She must have gone wrong.

No, wait. There was the sign. She swung into the parking lot and stopped. Gently scooping up her small charge, she half-walked, half-ran through the sliding doors. The little girl had been so quiet in the car. Isobel shied away from the thoughts that hounded her. *Too late. You are too late.* A ragged breath—she was still alive. "Stay with me, OK? Life is not done with you yet, little Flotsam."

Professionalism vaguely masked the disapproval on the receptionist's face. "Can we help you?"

Isobel was suddenly aware of her bare, sandy feet, mussed-up ponytail, and ripped shorts. "Please. I found this little girl on the beach. She needs urgent medical attention."

"Where are her parents?"

"I don't know. She was alone. Please—"

The receptionist tapped her pen on the form. "I have to put something here. The liability—"

Isobel's blood boiled. "But she needs help now!"

A cool hand grasped her elbow. It was the doctor. "I'll take it from here, Angie. I'm Doctor Brigham. Come with me."

She followed her rescuer, her knees weak from anger and gratitude. This baby dying in her arms? She swallowed hard. Her insides shook, pleading *no*. It wouldn't have surprised Isobel to see wings sprouting from the doctor's broad shoulders or a hovering halo to appear above his head.

He settled the little girl in a casualty booth. Assessing her vitals, he hooked up a drip and put monitoring equipment in place. Once his small patient was stable, he turned to Isobel. "OK... I think you got her here in time. She is suffering severe dehydration and sunburn. I'm not sure she would have survived another hour out there. We'll be able to assess her condition more accurately once she comes around. I've given her something to ease the pain." He sat on the bench next to Isobel. "What can you tell me?"

For the first time since her find, Isobel slammed back into reality. She cringed. "Not much to tell. I was on the beach and heard a strange moaning. I followed the sound and found her tied to a piece of driftwood like a bit of flotsam." She shrugged, hit by crushing weariness.

"No sign of her parents?"

"Just a pair of sandals halfway between where I found her and the water. I didn't want to waste time looking. I didn't think she had much time to spare."

"Good call. Tied to a piece of driftwood, you say?

With what?"

"A silk scarf. Bright red." A wave of nausea hit Isobel and she swallowed hard. "I need a bathroom."

Doctor Brigham waved toward the passage and she ran.

For the second time that morning nausea hit. She made it just in time and lost the entire contents of her stomach to the Sunshine Coast sewage system. She knelt, leaning on the wall, feeling hollow inside and out. The sooner she left this all behind, the better. Flotsam—Flo as she'd begun to think of her—was safe. Isobel had done as much as any decent person would. For the sake of conscience, she'd pay the bill, then she'd be out of here. This was not something she was ready to face. Not at all. Taking courage from the thought that it was almost over, she pulled herself up, splashed water on her face and opened the restroom door.

Dr. Brigham was waiting for her in the passage. For the briefest flash, Isobel saw the man—not the doctor, and her heartbeat doubled. She shook her head, and he was back to being the doctor, albeit with her conjured-up wings and halo hovering over his red hair. He looked worried.

"Is everything OK? Is she…"

"She's fine. As good as she can be under the circumstances. I'd like a word with you, if you don't mind."

"I was just going to settle the bill and be on my way. There is nothing more for me to do here."

"Just walk with me first. Please."

Isobel didn't want to. She didn't want to listen or feel. She just wanted to go home and stick her head under a pillow and pretend she was safely on the moon for a little while. Preferably alone. Yet she found her feet following him down a polished passage so shiny, it felt as if she were walking on the ceiling.

Those broad shoulders—with rapidly shrinking wings, she thought with a frown—nudged open a side door into a consulting room that had been left at the mercy of a colour-blind painter. Everything was green. His red hair blazed against the vivid emerald background. Her stomach was still queasy and the moon was sounding more attractive by the minute.

"I'm sorry, I never caught your name?" He waved her into a chair and sat down opposite her.

"Isobel. Isobel Carter."

"Isobel, I need to ask you—"

There was a brief tap on the door and sour Angie poked her head in. "Doctor, you have a growing queue of patients waiting to see you."

"Thank you, Angie. I'm nearly through."

He shook his head apologetically as the door slammed shut behind her. "She's good at what she does..." He shrugged, closed his mouth, and gave up trying to defend his untoward receptionist.

"You were saying?"

"Ah, yes. I need to ask if you'll do something for me."

No! "Sure." Traitorous mouth. "What is it?" She felt the need to bang her head on the desk. She resisted.

"That little girl you brought in. She needs to be in hospital, at least overnight. I know you said you were keen to get out of here, but will you take her?"

"I really can't. I mus—"

"I'd take her myself, but I've got a waiting room full of people. Please?"

"Can't you call ambulance?"

"None available, I tried. There was a pile-up on the N2."

She wanted to scream. *Hospital*. She could feel the trembling in her hands at the thought. "To hospital and then I'm done. Sure."

He reached across the desk and gently took hold of her wrist. "Stay with her until I do my rounds later. It's important. Please."

If he hadn't been so kind, she would have told him to get lost. But his hand on her wrist was warm, he asked so sincerely, and he looked her straight in the eye as he said it. Snookered. "OK. I'll take her and I'll wait for you. You had better not be late." His halo had slipped and she was tempted to strangle him with it.

"Good girl. I'll send someone to help you get her into your car. Oh, take this," he scribbled a note on a pad, tore it off, and handed it to her. "They won't give you trouble admitting her. I'm footing the bill on this one." He grinned at her, winked, and jogged off down the passage to fetch his next patient and appease the wrath of Angie.

Isobel leaned back on the chair and let her head drop. This could not be happening. *Pull yourself together, girl. It's just one afternoon. You can do this.* She wasn't really on speaking terms with God, but she looked up anyway.

Just don't let her die on me. Anything but that.

****

Liam Brigham shut the door to his consulting room, picked up the phone, and dialled.

"Detective Nass speaking."

"We've got another one."

"Missing?"

"No, intercepted. She's en route to hospital as we speak. We've got to talk."

2

Dr. Brigham must have phoned ahead. An elderly porter opened the door as Isobel pulled into the hospital parking lot. He moved with the telltale efficiency of one who'd spent many years handling broken bodies. He shifted Flo onto a stretcher and set up a mobile drip. He led on into the labyrinth of dim passages that reeked of strong disinfectant.

Something about that smell made Isobel glad she wasn't a malevolent micro-organism. Her mind took in random details as they walked. Generic pastel watercolours dotted the walls at regular intervals, the kind of pictures her art mentor from school would have used to line his parrot cage. The porter picked up the pace, giving her no time to think. She all but ran to keep up. They steered past the general ward and stopped in a private room.

With deft gentleness, he shifted Flo onto the bed and hung the drip. "Cover her with that sheet, will you?"

The sheet was soft and cool. Isobel pulled it over Flo and gingerly tucked it close under the little girl's chin. Like a doll in a giant's house, her damaged body barely took up any room, and Isobel felt her heart pull in a familiar ache. With the ache came another wave of nausea. She found a chair and doubled over, head between her knees, willing it to pass.

"Are you OK, Ma'am?"

Nodding as convincingly as she could, Isobel managed to look up long enough to squeeze out a vague smile.

"All right, then. All the best with your little mite. She's a fighter, she is. Just like her mom." He gave her shoulder an encouraging pat.

Isobel cringed, but the thought of explaining the situation meant opening her mouth, and that meant she may well throw up on the porter's worn sneakers. She forced another grin which must have come out as a grimace.

He took one look and left.

Alone with Flo, Isobel breathed to stay calm. The sun was surrendering to night, and the light through the window took on a magical pink-orange glow that made her think of flamingos. She couldn't bring herself to look at Flo; her fierce redness made Isobel's skin crawl. How could one little girl stir up so much emotion?

Isobel got up and sought the coolness of the window with her aching forehead. So many unanswered questions—a riddle waiting to be untangled like a ball of thread. But with that unravelling, memories would shake loose, she knew it. Memories she'd do anything to avoid. Memories that threatened to swallow her up and spit out her bones.

The room looked out over the town's main road, lined with dolphin-peddling curio shops and fast-food outlets. Life happened at a mellow pace in Scottburgh, South Africa. Off-season was particularly laidback, a quality that drew in many visitors from the busier centres over holiday season.

Bel had heard locals joke about spotting outsiders on the beaches by their pale, office-bound skin or the sunburn that they inevitably wore after two days on holiday.

The wind picked up, no longer teasing the palm trees, but determined to shred them. Riding the tails of the wind were thick, black storm clouds. In minutes, the flamingo light had fled from an onslaught of pelting rain.

Isobel cringed. Her canvas was still on the beach. Easel, paints...her shoes. In this rain? It would all be ruined. Perfect. Just perfect.

The door swung open and a nurse came in to check Flo's vitals.

Time turned sticky as Isobel stared at the open door. She could leave. Right now. Flo was in good hands. Isobel owed Dr. Brigham nothing.

Blood rushed to her face as she stood up and walked. Every slow step was a pounding heartbeat. *I told him I'd stay, but I can't.* Her pace quickened as she got closer to the door. Fighting the urge to run, Isobel fled the hospital like an ant fleeing a kid with a magnifying glass on a sunny day.

Taxis lined the street. Rush-hour in this holiday town was a non-event. She slid into one, and two stops later she arrived at her rented cottage with her ruined canvas and a steaming packet of Chinese food that was her best attempt at supper. She settled in the lounge with her noodles and tea, determined to shift-delete today from her memory banks.

I made the right decision. There was nothing more I could do for that baby. I wouldn't survive anything more.

Not hungry, Isobel forced herself to keep lifting the plastic fork from the greasy cardboard to her mouth. Somewhere between the warm liquid and the sweet and sour tang of the noodles, the clutch let up in her mind and tension dissolved from her shoulders. Her gaze fell on the canvas—watermarked from the rain, beach sand embedded along the edges. Her stomach twisted and she set the half-eaten noodles aside. Maybe bed would be best.

She lay in her bed in the dark and listened to the wind. The storm had vented its fury for an hour solid then left as quickly as it had come. It took half an hour of turning this way and that, re-fluffing her pillow, to realise that she was fooling herself. Her good friend sleep was off visiting in another part of the town and had no intention of coming back anytime soon.

Throwing on a silk gown, Isobel wandered downstairs. The wind had blown away the last lingering remnants of rain clouds and tucked itself in for the night.

Moonlight poured through the ceiling-length windows, creating a pool of living light on the lounge floor. Driven by some nameless emotion, Isobel picked up the ruined canvas and a pencil. She stood for a moment outside the circle of dancing moonlight, feeling suspended between the life that is and the life that will be.

She stepped into the glow and sank to the floor. Without really intending to, she slowly began to sketch. No thoughts dictated where the lines went or the shading grew. The pencil tip traced and dipped, at times light—barely touching—then bold and dark. Time flowed over her under the caress of soft moonlight as she gave in to the whim of her overwhelming feelings. Feelings she dare not look at in the harsh light of day. She worked tirelessly, pouring her heart out through her finger tips, redeeming the damaged canvas with exquisite beauty.

Hours later, needle-sharp pricks of sunlight woke her up. She struggled upright, feeling every vertebra in her spine mumbling complaints.

Oh, hush up already, body. What are you doing on the floor anyway?

Rubbing thick sleep from her eyes, she forced them open—first one then the other. Then she saw the canvas.

Ten years of nothing. Ten long years of bashing her head on empty canvas after empty canvas and now this.

A tremor of shock shot through her from the tip of her head to the deepest secret places of her heart. It was suddenly hard to swallow. The form, the lines, the shading and contrast—it was, without doubt, the best piece she'd ever done.

And...it was Flo.

3

She stowed the damaged canvas next to the dustbin—the picture facing towards the wall—and was on her second cup of tea when she heard the crash.

Someone screamed. Then silence.

Running to the window, she moved the lace curtain aside just enough to peep into the neighbour's yard without being seen.

A bike, a boy, a gate that hung precariously on one hinge, and a battered daisy bush told the tale of a crash.

Her neighbour's front door swung open. The boy's mom ran and bent down over him. With her hair scraped back into a spiky ponytail and something pink messed down the back of her track pants, she was an overworked mom through and through.

The boy cried and clutched his arm.

Isobel let the curtain drop. *Not my problem.*

Popping two slices of seed bread into the toaster, she opened the top drawer before remembering the cutlery was in the next one down. *You'd think I'd be used to this place after a month.* A whole month of living in Scottburgh and she'd managed to avoid meeting her neighbours. Waving the butter knife in midair, she said aloud, "I'm not here to make friends, after all. I'm just here to hunt down my missing muse. Nothing more, nothing less."

The toaster popped loudly, the only applause she

was going to get for her soliloquy.

She spread a thick layer of marmalade across her toast and was about to bite when the doorbell rang. She rolled her eyes. *Perfect.* She put the toast down on the bookshelf in the hall, brushed crumbs from her hands, and peered through the spy-hole.

A spiky blonde ponytail told her it was the next-door mom. The soft crying told her bike-boy was there too. It would be so easy to slip quietly into the lounge and lay low until they gave up and left. So tempting.

She opened the door.

"I need your help. He's broken his arm. My hubby's away. My car won't start. I—"

This can't be happening. "Give me a mo'. I need my keys." She slipped into her shoes, found her keys, and left with a last wistful glance at her toast. Then it hit her.

"Oh, crumbs. My car isn't here. How can I be so dim?"

Blonde mom blinked, uncomprehending.

The boy buried his head in his mom's leg and whimpered.

Isobel sighed. "You know what? It doesn't matter. I'll call a taxi."

Minutes later, they were trading names as they piled into the back of the yellow vehicle. The boy's name was Ben, and he apparently had ongoing issues with staying on his bike.

"Oh, Ben, how many times have I told you to use your brakes *before* you hit the gate? You really need to stop falling off that bike. You've only got so many limbs to break, you know." Ben's mom kept up a nonstop stream of chatter, chiding and consoling, interjected with the odd comment to Isobel. "So kind of you to help. I wish my husband didn't travel as much as he does, but what can you do?"

Through it all, Isobel found out that Melindi, the sobbing boy's mom, had a six-month-old baby girl at home with her nanny and a hubby that travelled out of town. A lot.

"Do you know he is away nearly half of the year?"

They pulled up outside the hospital, saving Isobel from having to answer. She moved to safer ground. "Would you like me to wait for you?"

Ben clutched his arm and sobbed.

Melindi's eyes took on a vague panic. "Please walk us in? I'm not sure I'll manage doors carrying him."

Come on, universe! Give me a break! "I really can't—"

"It's OK. I'll get by." Melindi slid out the car with Ben in her arms, but the movement twisted his arm.

He screamed and started crying with fresh gusto.

"Wait! Melindi, sit tight. I'll go get a wheelchair."

Melindi didn't answer, but nodded. Her eyes were moist with unshed tears, the strain beginning to show in the creases on her forehead.

The nightshift and dayshift nursing staff were trading places as they walked into casualty. A dayshifter met them at the front desk. "Hey, Ben! What do we have here, Mel?"

"Ben fell off his bike again. This time I'm sure he's broken his arm."

"Right. Let's get you straight to x-ray. Follow me."

Isobel trailed after the wheelchair feeling like a sixth finger. *Who on earth is on first name terms with the emergency staff in casualty?* She shook her head in wonder and kept walking. Every step took them closer to the paediatric ward.

By the time the radiologist took over, Melindi was

shaking. "My nerves are shot."

"You need some caffeine. I'll go find us some coffee."

Melindi frowned at her trembling hands and slumped into a plastic chair that looked more tired than she did. "That would be great. Thank you, Bel. For everything."

Isobel didn't trust herself to answer. She smiled faintly and went on a hunt for coffee. She found it—right outside Flo's room. Curiosity put her hand to the door, and she pushed it open before she'd given it a second thought. Then she froze. Hand on the door handle, one foot in the room...she was stuck. Stepping over the threshold was impossible. *Can't do this. Fool!* She spun around to leave and walked smack into Dr. Brigham.

"You came back! Come and see. She woke up earlier this morning." He grabbed her arm and pulled her into the room, ignoring the deep furrows in the tile caused by her reluctant heels.

A nurse was wiping down Flo with a cool cloth and the child whimpered at every touch.

Isobel's heart lurched.

A lopsided grin tugged at the doctor's lips. "It's OK." His voice was gentle.

Isobel wasn't sure if he was talking to her or to Flo.

The nurse moved aside, clearing a space Isobel dreaded filling.

The good doctor brought her forward and she felt an overwhelming urge to accidentally grind her heel into his foot. Then she looked at Flo. The angry red had deepened since the night before, much like a tomato ripe enough to burst. Blisters had already begun forming.

Her eyes were open, though unfocussed.

"She's a bit out of it from the pain meds." He reached up and checked the flow from her drip. "I've also put her on an antibiotic. Infection would be bad news. Her little system is under so much strain as it is." He leaned on the bed, moving close enough to look into the little girl's eyes.

She responded with a clumsy hand on his cheek.

He cupped her hand in his and smiled as the nurse packed up her swabs, bowl, and towels and left.

His eyes never strayed from the girl who continued to pat his cheek, but his words were for Isobel. "It is good that you came back. I thought I'd lost you for a while last night."

She had no idea what to say to that. Saying nothing at all seemed to be working for her. She stuck with it.

"Her name is Mia."

"Oh?"

"Label on her clothes." He gestured towards a pink bundle of folded cotton on the shelf next to the bed.

Mia's eyelids grew heavy and her breathing slowed a touch as she drifted into peaceful sleep.

Isobel found herself mesmerized by the rise and fall of the child's chest. Somehow, it fed some empty space inside of her that she'd shoved in a dusty corner and ignored for years.

"I need to finish my rounds but I also need to talk to you. About Mia. She needs a safe place to stay for a while." He pulled a card from his pocket.

Isobel said a mental 'Ha!' at the thought of getting off so lightly.

Cards get lost. Cards get forgotten in pockets and

ruined in the wash. She could think of thirty reasons why she'd never have to make the call without breaking a sweat. There was no way she was taking in a toddler.

Then he pulled a pen from the other pocket and asked, "Number please?"

Her insides groaned.

"I'm in hurry. What is your number?"

The man was pure, 100 percent bully. "I'm staying in Breezy Cottage just off the beachfront. The number is in the book."

"Great. I'll be in touch. The name is Liam, by the way."

By the time she got back to Melindi with two steaming cups, Ben was moving from x-ray to a consulting room. The novelty of riding in a wheelchair took his mind off the pain enough to put a broad grin on his face.

Melindi took the cup and swallowed two big gulps. "This is just what I need. Where have you been all my life?"

"Is it broken?"

"Oh yeah. Doc says it's a clean break though. Should heal perfectly. Six weeks in a cast for a busy eight-year-old. This is not going to be fun."

It was midday by the time they walked out into bright sunshine.

Ben sported his new cast proudly and ran along tapping it on each dustbin, pole, or person they passed, eliciting a frazzled "Ben! Stop that!" from his mom with every clang.

The irritation that had been building since her run-in with the doctor dissolve as Ben swung around and grinned at them. His eyes danced, and he ran at full speed and barrelled into his mom, nearly knocking her off her feet. "Sorry, Mommy!" Then he was off again, swinging his arm as if to check if it would fall off.

Melindi frowned. "Just wait until the pain meds wear off. Poor kid."

That's the trouble with the numbness that sets in after great pain: it always wears off. Isobel sighed. "Let's get you two home." She found her car just where she'd left it the night before. Melindi raised an eyebrow.

"Don't even ask."

****

The restlessness hit again without warning. Isobel scrubbed the kitchen floor on her knees with a nail brush as her scrubbing brush had deserted her, then found a dusty spot behind the fridge that required advanced yoga skills to get to. The sun was losing its grip on the horizon as she emptied the cutlery drawer and soaped down the divider tray.

The doorbell rang.

Rubbing an itch on her forehead with the back of her dripping hand, she opened the door and clung to the handle as her knees nearly gave way. "Dr. Brigham. You didn't phone." She cringed even as the words bungeed off her lips.

"Please don't Dr. Brigham me, just call me Liam. No, I didn't phone. I had an unexpected gap and thought I'd come find you instead of…calling." He didn't look the slightest bit apologetic.

"Well, I can make tea if you want to come in. Though I'm sure you are busy…"

"No. Yes! I mean…I'd like tea. I'm not rushing." His eyes were twinkling and he coughed behind his hand. She could swear he was trying not to laugh.

"I'll put the kettle on then." What was going on with this man? She steered him to the lounge and put the light on in the kitchen to make up for the failing sun. Bending down to take two cups from the cupboard, she saw her reflection in the toaster. A stray lock of hair trailed down her forehead, sporting a row of sparkly soap bubbles. So the man found soap bubbles funny. She slapped her forehead, sending the residue flying. This was not going well.

She carried the tea through, wishing for a giant fast forward button. The lounge seemed smaller with him in it. She put his cup down and tackled his chuckling head on. "So you find soapy foreheads funny?"

"No, not at all."

She felt her eyebrow climb. *Oh, really?*

"What really makes me chuckle, though, are those." He pointed to two perfectly round dirty marks on her knees. "Nice homey touch."

She looked at her knees, promptly fell off the edge of mortification, and landed in the lap of so-what. She grinned with a shrug. "I clean floors, and I've got the knees to prove it. Have you got a problem with that?" She sat on the sofa opposite and fluffed the cushion next to her. She pointedly left her dirty knees just as they were.

He chuckled. "Not at all. In fact, why don't you come over and clean mine next?"

Isobel had grown up with three brothers and knew how to defend herself. She picked up the cushion and threw it across the room. Hard. It hit him as he took a sip of tea, slopping hot liquid into his lap.

"Oh, grief! I'm sorry! Here let me help—"

"You have got some serious muscles on you, woman. Relax, I'll mop up in the kitchen." He stepped gingerly across the carpet like a cat in snow, trying to stop the liquid pool in his shirt from dripping on the floor.

Isobel wished she could disappear into a parallel universe in which she had never met, nor thrown cushions at, Dr. Liam Brigham. She rose to help him clean up as a good hostess should, thought about what that involved, and promptly did the right thing—took her tea and escaped to the deck.

Moonlight shimmered across the broad expanse of sea. The salty air was cool around her. A fresh breeze had picked up since the sun had set.

She heard him come back and turned around to see if he'd been successful in his tea-mopping efforts.

He stood frozen in the middle of the lounge. He held the picture of Flo—little Mia—in one hand, the other across his forehead, hiding his eyes—his feelings.

Her heart caught in her throat. "What are you doing with that?" She moved to take it out of his hands, but he dodged.

"Where did you get this?"

"That is none of your business." His tone raised her defences, and she reacted much as a bear would if poked with a stick.

He dropped his hand and she read turmoil in his eyes. It made no sense.

"I'm sorry, Isobel." He sounded tired, impatient. "I don't mean to pry. It's just that I want to know the truth about her. I thought you weren't connected to her in any way. But this?" He floundered, trying to find the right words, "This goes against everything you've said. Tell me the truth, Isobel. Please."

Anger flared. "You are assuming many things. Things you know nothing about."

"Well, then, tell me what is really going on."

"You actually think I'm involved with this?" She took the sketch from his hands and clutched it to her chest. She crossed the hall and opened the front door without a word. It was time for him to leave.

He didn't. He stood in the middle of the hallway. "Talk to me, Bel."

She hid behind her crumbling anger, desperately trying to stay mad. "Don't call me Bel. Just go."

"I can't do that. For her sake, I can't. Talk to me."

She fought the tears that threatened. "I won't. Please."

"No." One word, spoken so softly. A mountain that simply would not yield. "Talk to me."

She sank to the floor, her back against the cool cement of the wall. The sketch of Mia fell to her feet, and she turned it face-down. There was only one way to get rid of this man. "I'm an artist. I lost it...somehow. For the last ten years, I've been trying to find it again. That's why I'm here in Scottburgh. I haven't been able to paint or draw anything. That night, after I'd taken her to hospital, I couldn't sleep. I came down here and drew that by moonlight."

"The canvas is damaged. Why—?"

"I left it at the beach when I brought her in. The storm got to it before I did. I don't know the whys and hows, Liam. All I know is that she is the first thing that I've managed to get out on paper in a decade."

He came and slid down the wall opposite her, feet next to hers, reaching across the narrow passage. He picked up the sketch of Mia and propped it on his lap, studying every detail. "She's not the first abandoned baby you know."

"Of course not. I know that."

"I don't mean in general. I'm talking about right here, in Scottburgh, over the last eighteen months. She is the third that I know of." He looked Isobel straight in the eye.

She saw something in his expression that twisted her gut though she couldn't say why. Her gaze dropped to her hands on her knees.

He carried on, "I've tried to trace the other two through the foster system, and I've gotten nowhere. I'm not convinced they've been well placed. I don't know that they are safe."

"And their moms? Dads?"

"The other two were single moms. Both suicide cases. Something is not right here. Mia needs a safe place."

Isobel reached over and took the picture out of his hands. "Why does it matter to you?"

"It just does. That's beside the point. This little girl needs you."

"You don't know what you are asking." She fought to stop the trembling in her suddenly cold hands. *I don't do babies. I can't.*

He switched sides, sitting close to her. She could feel the warmth from his arm on her bare skin. "Just think about it. That's all I'm asking."

"Fine."

Liam opened his mouth as if he was about to say more, closed it, and bumped shoulders with her. "Thanks for the tea"—he held out his soggy shirt—"and the swim. It was fun. We should do it again."

Isobel cringed. "I have a better idea. Let's *not* do that again."

"Ha! Where's your sense of adventure anyway?" His sudden grin was broad. It masked the emotion in his eyes and disarmed her completely. "I must be on my way. I'll be in touch." He got up and held out his hands to help her off the floor.

She put her hands in his without thinking. Warmth filled her.

"Oh! Just so you know—visiting hours don't apply to you because she's in a private room."

Like a bucket of ice water on a fire. Fizzle. She wanted to smack him. "You don't know when to stop, do you?"

He ignored her. "Anytime, really. Just pop in."

She glared at him and tilted her head to the open door.

"I mean it, anytime."

"Oh, please. Just go!"

****

Liam removed his shoes and rolled his shoulders to warm up the muscles. He picked up a lime-green bowling ball and hoisted it in front of himself to test the weight. Music pumped through the room. Why Nass couldn't just find a dark corner of a restaurant was beyond him, then again...the noise level was perfect for clandestine conversation.

Detective Rupert Nass came through the door, his gaze scanning each lane of bowlers. He smiled when he found Liam. Shorter than Liam and without a scrap of extra body fat, he moved with restless energy.

The two old school chums had spent their senior years vying over top marks in the grade, and each found a lifelong friend in the process.

Nass wasted no time picking out a steel grey ball. "I'm going to thrash you today."

Liam slapped him on the shoulder, "Good to see you too, mate."

Nass's first throw took out eight pins. "So, what's up?"

Liam released a ball. Six pins fell. "It's time for the police to step in and do their job. It can't go on like this. Have you found the worm in your apple yet?"

"Brigs, I've narrowed it down to three guys I don't trust. It's going to take time. Tell me about the intercept."

Liam faced his friend, feeling the weight of the ball in his palm. "We're out of time. How many more kids must disappear before you make a move?"

"I'm as frustrated as you. Tell me about the intercept."

"A two-year-old was brought in by a woman, an artist. Same set up. She found the child on the beach tied up with a red scarf. The beach was deserted, no sign of parents. The girl is in stable condition in hospital. If not for the kindness of a stranger, she'd be another number on your books right now. You need to find the insider, and you need to do it now."

Nass let fly. Gutter ball. He stood silent for a moment and then turned. "To be frank, I don't want my guys anywhere near this little girl until I know who I can trust. I need you to buy me some time. A couple of days. Do whatever you have to. If this blows up, I'll take the heat."

4

The flea market was a sprawling expanse of texture, colour, and noise that would take a full day to explore from one end to the other.

Isobel retied her laces and settled her backpack between her shoulder blades. She was keen to spend the day doing just that.

It was barely 8 AM, but the sun was up-and-at-'em like a lifeguard on duty at a toddlers' pool.

Her cottage was clean, the canvasses were blank, and Isobel's head was full of thoughts she'd rather not think. The flea market was a welcome distraction.

Incense hung thick in the air around the first stall. The clothing on offer was hand dyed in India, soft saris with embroidery in rich jewel colours. She moved on. Africa-inspired animal prints themed the next stall. Cushions with black and white zebra stripes, cheetah-spotted rugs, lampshades from delicate ostrich eggs.

Isobel kept walking. She stopped once to buy a fruit smoothie, then on again, sipping cold liquid through a straw and allowing her surroundings to permeate her senses, to flood her soul. The taste of summer berries lingered on her tongue.

In a corner of the market, a white tent hung suspended over long tables set up for a craft workshop. Fifteen adults bent over mosaic creations in various stages of completion. A slim lady in black flitted between them like a restless butterfly, tweaking a shard of mirror here, adjusting a blue tile there—guiding her students into perfection of their craft. She had a shock of red hair that bobbed as she moved. Samples of the artwork created in the tent hung at intervals along the edge of the space.

Isobel found herself drawn in, studying each piece critically. A sapphire and emerald swirling piece with a seashell as its focal point made her smile. It was simple but effective, cleverly done.

"Incredible how something so broken can be so beautiful, isn't it?"

Isobel turned.

The red-head teacher stood behind her, her gaze firmly fixed on the seashell piece.

Isobel nodded, not answering.

"What makes it beautiful is how each piece catches the light and reflects it in its own unique way."

"True. I've never thought about it like that."

"Have you ever done mosaic work?"

"It was one of the subjects I enjoyed most at art school."

"Aaah! A true artist. I knew it. I can spot these things you know. My name is Rochelle de Lange."

"Isobel."

"Well, my dear Isobel. Come and see what we're up to."

Isobel settled in a chair as a grey-haired student called for help.

Rochelle leaned over her student to position a fragment of mirror, "*Ow!*" The sharp edge of the mirror had sliced a deep gash in her finger. "I think I hit a vein. This is a real gusher."

The student dug in her bag for a tissue. "Will this help?"

Rochelle wrapped her finger, but the tissue soaked through in seconds. "Thanks, Dotty, but I'm going to have to find a plaster." She looked over to Isobel with a questioning shrug of her shoulders, "Everybody—this is Isobel. She is an artist. If you need help while I'm gone—you can ask her. OK?"

The question was for Isobel, who took one look at the bright red tissue and nodded. "We'll be fine. Off you go!"

"I'll come with you, Roch," said an elegant lady with a sleek brown bob. "You shouldn't go by yourself."

They left quickly leaving Isobel facing fourteen pairs of eyes, all looking at her and blinking like owls in the dark.

She did the only thing she knew how to do. "Anybody stuck?"

A petite, blonde twenty-something stuck her hand up. "I have a duck here that looks more like a bread roll. Help?"

The group chuckled as Isobel went over. The next forty-five minutes flew by as she rescued Miriam's ducks, corrected the angle of Suzy's mirror waterfall, and helped Joe choose colours to suit a stained-glass-inspired piece for his granddaughter. A strange peace filled Isobel as she tackled troubles of small consequence. Other people's troubles, not her own. Troubles she was able to fix.

Rochelle came back, flustered. "I'm so sorry, people! We walked forever before we found plasters, then the ATM was out of cash. One thing after the next. What a nightmare! Anyway! How are you all doing?" She took a quick walk between the two tables, casting a sharp eye on each one's progress. "This looks good!"

In his slow drawl, Joe said, "She ain't you, Miss Rochelle, but this Isobel? She's the next best thing, she is."

"I'm so glad it worked. Thank you, Isobel! Right everyone, that's it for today. We'll be back tomorrow at the same time to finish these off." She grabbed Isobel's arm just as she was leaving. "I'm looking for someone to help me teach. My daughter has just had twins." She smiled a little wearily. "I want to be free on occasion to be Grandma. Think about it." She pressed a small purple business card into Isobel's hands.

"Sure." *No way*.

"You know where to find us."

5

Isobel unlocked the door to her cottage. She felt light for the first time in forever. She even hummed a bit of a half-forgotten song that stuck with her from when she was little. Maybe moving here had been a good decision after all.

She poured mango juice into a tall glass and unpacked her bag. Right at the bottom was Rochelle's business card. Instead of throwing it away, she found herself sticking it up with a sickly yellow banana fridge magnet right next to Liam's. *Doesn't mean I'm actually going to call.*

A warm puddle of sunlight drew her to the couch closest to the sliding door. She settled in, tucked her feet under her, and sipped slowly, savouring the quiet.

The rude buzz of the doorbell ripped through the silence.

Isobel jerked, slopping sticky mango over her hand. "What now?" She peered through the spy-hole.

Melindi peered back, this time with baby and all.

Isobel slid back the heavy bolt, resisting the urge to lick her sticky hand, and opened the door.

Ben clutched his mom's leg with his good arm. He sported a whopping shiner around his left eye. He stared at the floor, his normal cheeky grin replaced with the ashen face of a dead man walking.

The baby on Melindi's hip was red in the face and crying.

Melindi looked as if she might cry too. "I need help," she shouted, to make herself heard over the crying.

Isobel managed to keep the sympathetic face glued on through sheer willpower. A thousand excuses flowered and died in her mind. "What's going on?"

"Ben got into a fight at school. The headmaster phoned, he wants to—" She shifted the squirming baby to the other hip and dropped the nappy bag on Ben's foot.

The tin of formula hit with a crack, and Ben's eyes filled with tears. He buried his face in her leg again and sobbed.

She bent down to soothe him and nearly dropped the baby, who doubled her screaming efforts. "He wants to see us. But I can't take Lilly, and my help didn't show up."

Isobel's mind ran. *Alone with a crying baby? Heck no!*

Yet Melindi stood like a palm tree in the middle of a hurricane, each arm full of a crying kid. Only palm trees didn't have tears running down their cheeks.

"Give her here. It will be fine." She felt her palms go sweaty even as the words left her mouth.

"You sure? I just don't know what else to do."

"It's fine, really."

"I don't know how to thank you." Melindi handed over the nappy bag. "She'll need a bottle in about half an hour. Just add water and shake. Everything you might need is in this bag." She kissed Lilly's fluff-covered head and handed the screaming child to Isobel. "We'll be back as soon as possible." With a worried backward glance, she took Ben and left.

Lilly screamed flat out for the next hour.

Isobel tried everything. She walked outside with her in the warm sunshine, then worried that the rest of the neighbours might be wondering who was being murdered, so she hurried back inside. She sat the child on the bed and played peek-a-boo.

Lilly didn't like it and fell backwards weeping her objections.

Isobel made the bottle…Lilly flung it across the room. It landed in the washing basket with frightening accuracy.

Isobel began to wonder whether she should throw a spectacular tantrum of her own and cry louder than Lilly. Maybe it would have some effect. It was only the pounding headache that had lodged itself in the base of her skull that stopped her. She did the only thing she knew would calm her shattered nerves. Put the kettle on. Tea first. Nervous breakdown after.

"Sorry, kiddo. I really need to get rid of this sticky hand." Isobel had been through the entire Lilly saga sporting her *eau de la* mango juice. With Lilly on her hip, she turned the tap on to rinse it.

Lilly stopped crying as if someone had flicked her switch. She leaned out of Isobel's arms and reached for the water. It trickled over her fingers, and she chuckled, though her eyelashes were still wet with tears.

Isobel was shocked. She ran the water a little faster.

Lilly leaned way over, trying to catch the stream with two hands.

Isobel sat her on the sink with her feet in the basin, water within reach. Lilly shrieked with glee and clapped her hands sending water flying. She gasped with each cold drop that hit her face. Could this be the same baby who would have given an ambulance a run for its money mere minutes ago? It didn't take long for her clothes to be soaked through. It was a small price to pay.

Isobel drank her cup of tea in peace and figured it was time to try the bottle again. She braced herself and turned the tap off.

On cue, Lilly started crying. Moving as quickly as humanly possible, she changed Lilly into dry clothes, nearly getting her head through the arm hole twice before it popped through the right hole.

Lilly helped by wriggling as much as she knew how and letting out heartbroken wails at regular intervals.

The pounding in Isobel's head had levelled up to a sledgehammer and seemed intent on cracking her skull open. Between the noise and the stress of managing this little six-month-old dictator, she didn't stand a chance.

Retrieving the bottle from the laundry basket, she picked up Lilly's blanket with her toes, transferred it to the same hand that held the bottle and walked out back to the swing bench trying not to drop any of her cargo. An ancient flowering frangipani tree hung umbrella-like over the swing, throwing random patterns of dappled shade and light. Two swings for one house seemed extravagant, but Isobel liked it.

She tucked Lilly firmly in her arms, fumbled to get the blanket over her, and put the bottle to the child's mouth, before kicking off the grass to get the swing moving.

Lilly fought long enough to let out a few more obligatory sobs in protest, then took to the bottle and quieted down, drinking furiously. Before long, the movement of the swing took effect and her eyelids grew heavy. Her sucking slowed, her breathing deepened, and the weight of her tiny body shifted as she relaxed. She drew one last shuddery breath and slipped off to sleep.

Isobel sat still, too scared to move, letting the motion of the swing come to a natural stop. She put the bottle down on the swing next to her and decided against wiping the milk from the corners of Lilly's mouth. There was something magical in this moment. A wave of thorough contentment washed over her, sitting on the swing holding a sleeping baby. If only this was real, this peace, this joy. Isobel felt herself breathe—truly breathe!—again.

Seconds later, unavoidable in its wake, a rough wave of jagged memory crashed down on her, smothering her beneath its terrible weight, threatening to rip through her soul.

The baby in her arms played catalyst, and she sat in the speckled twilight—neither in the light, nor in the dark and wept for what could have been.

For the life that had been stolen from her.

6

As the sun rose, Isobel made up her mind. After another night of fitful sleep that did nothing more than put creases in her sheets, she knew it was time to move on. She took a headache pill from a bottle in the cupboard, thought for a moment and took another. It took a whole glass of water to wash away the bitter taste.

This place was not working out. The only creative spark she'd found tied her to a tangled mess of painful, unanswered questions and dark places in her soul she had no desire to revisit.

She ran a cloth over the counter-top, glanced out the window, and sighed. It's not every kitchen that looks out over the sea. That, she'd miss. The rest of it? *I can do without all this drama.*

Melindi had fetched Lilly shortly after she'd fallen asleep. The poor woman was so caught up in managing her own troubles that she hadn't noticed Isobel's dire frame of mind. She'd gushed gratitude non-stop, while Isobel sported the fake "I'm OK" face that she had perfected so long ago. It worked its magic: Melindi had taken her baby and left with no awkward questions.

Between Mia, Lilly, and the bulldog of a doctor, it was all getting too much.

Isobel took her car keys off the hook in the passage. Nine AM was as a good a time as any to pick up some empty boxes to start packing. She'd already shut and locked the door when the phone rang. Any other person would have left it to ring. It was not in her genes to ignore a ringing phone. Letting herself back in, she ran and picked up. "I'm looking for Isobel."

"That's me. Who am I speaking to?"

"Lovey, Rochelle here. Are you busy today? I need your help with a decoupage class."

It took a moment for Isobel to place her. Aah, the crazy craft lady. "I'm sorry. I've got plans—"

"My dear, you don't understand. This is an emergency. I simply can't leave these people alone and unsupervised with sharp craft knives. They'll be slicing their own fingertips off. They need you."

Isobel found herself fighting the urge to giggle. Sliced fingertips, indeed.

"That's a dire situation you have right there, Rochelle. I'll have to postpone my plans then." One morning wouldn't make much difference; the boxes could wait for tomorrow. Maybe tonight she'd get some proper sleep, and packing would go even quicker.

"Good. I'll see you at nine forty-five at my downtown studio. Address is in the phone book under The Artist's Loft. Don't be late." She put the phone down cutting off the words poised on Isobel's tongue.

"OK, then. I guess I'll see you at nine forty-five." She replaced the receiver and leaned back, resting her head on the wall.

This felt like some evil conspiracy.

****

Rochelle's downtown studio was a second floor room big enough to comfortably handle a party of a few dozen rhinos. The ceiling boasted glass panels at regular intervals, letting in generous helpings of natural light.

Isobel let out a low whistle. Artists would bump each other off to work in a place like this. Stepping out of the lift for the first time, Isobel felt the flock of butterflies take flight in her belly.

This place was an oasis of inspiration. Scattered through the room, were original works of art, some complex and intricate, others breathtaking in their simplicity. Tables were set up in groups, with an entire wall dedicated to art supplies. Between that and the lift, the room buckled sideways into an alcove where an eclectic collection of works in various mediums and stages of completion dotted rows of shelves.

"You're here. Good. Follow me."

Without any ceremony, Isobel walked behind Rochelle, feeling a little in awe of this diminutive woman. In a flea market tent, she was a scatterbrained gypsy who peddled her talent to make a living. In this environment, she took on an entirely different persona: a true artist who had carved out the perfect space to create in.

"We've got ten minutes until the class arrives. Let me show you what's what." Rochelle moved through the space as if she were dancing to some strange beat in her head, hands gesturing toward this cupboard for cutting knives and boards, that one for decoupage medium and paint. Brushes lived in a tall cupboard by the window at the back of the room.

"The lesson is two hours. This is a new group so you'll have to walk them through the process step by step. The theme for this morning is faeries and fantasies. I will be back at noon to wrap up. Any questions?"

"Yes, in fact I do have one." Isobel thought about how to word this. "You don't know me at all. You know nothing about me. How is it that you trust me to walk in here and take over? Don't you need to see my résumé or something?"

Rochelle reached out and held Isobel's chin with a hand that smelled like marshmallows and stared deeply into her eyes. "I am never wrong about people. You need to be here." For the first time since they had met, Rochelle smiled. "You need to be here. Let's leave it at that for now." She patted Isobel's cheek, picked up her ostrich leather bag, and waved once as she left.

Within minutes, the lift bell dinged nonstop as ladies arrived, filling the air with chatter.

Isobel soon had her hands full of moms stealing a few hours from their domestic kingdoms to come and explore their creative sides.

Savannah came straight from gym and kept wrinkling her nose at her armpits as if she should have showered.

Maggie wore grey and hunched in the corner.

Jules had everything in perfect order, each strand of pale hair, every nail, even her clothes seemed thoroughly obedient—no speck or wrinkle. Impressive for a mom of twin boys.

Mischa arrived eating a chocolate bar. She was almost as wide as she was tall. She smiled at Isobel and hugged her. "It's so good to meet you."

For a brief moment, Isobel froze but the overwhelming warmth from this short lady melted her reservations and she found herself grinning back.

Kez-lyn was as scatter-brained as a room full of chickens. Within moments of arriving, she'd misplaced her keys, dropped her phone on the floor, and forgotten Isobel's name twice. She was also the first to commit fairy-cide.

Her mission was to decorate a tissue box for her fairy-besotted daughter, Kelsey. She'd chosen a willowy water fairy kneeling over a small pond from the pile of paper. Her blue hair was drawn up into a high pile on her head, with delicate ringlets trailing down her back. It was an exquisite image in every way, except for her neck. With the hair gone, it left her skinny little neck wide open to abuse. A slip of the craft knife was all it took to separate her head from her shoulders.

Isobel was leaning over Maggie's gift box when she heard the shriek. The image of severed fingers filled Isobel's mind as she swung around to see what happened.

"Oh, no! I've killed my fairy!" Kez-lyn's eyes were bulging in horror.

"Kez! My heart nearly stopped! Don't scream like that!" Savannah chided.

Maggie took it all in with a shake of her head and a wry smile.

Mischa was immediately sympathetic, "Oh, never mind, love. Plenty more where that one came from."

"I know, but it took ages to cut her out. Now I'll have to start again!"

Between them, they'd given Isobel enough time to recover. "Kez, we can fix it. Don't worry." With some careful use of the decoupage medium, Isobel managed to reunite Kez-lyn's fairy with her head. The sprite once more gazed serenely at herself in the pond.

Jules examined the patch-up job, "You're good. Seriously good."

There were no more beheadings and the morning flew by in a blur.

True to her word, Rochelle was back by noon to see them all off.

The lift shut, cutting off the sounds of the last few ladies laughing and chatting on their way out.

"So, how was that?" All traces of that smile were gone.

Isobel couldn't help feeling like a naughty schoolgirl caught in some misdemeanour. The feeling was so bizarre she fought hard not to laugh. "Actually that was great."

"You sound surprised."

"I guess I am. There hasn't been much that I've enjoyed for a long time."

"Good. Then you'll come back tomorrow?"

Before Isobel could protest, Rochelle ferreted around in her bag and came out with a wad of notes. "Payment for the two lessons you've taught. Hereafter, I'll pay you at the end of each week."

Isobel stood with the notes in her hand, a touch shell-shocked. Two hours ago she was leaving, now here she was—semi-employed. How on earth?

"Well, put that away before I assume you don't want it. Clean up and you're free to go. Your class tomorrow will be at two. Be here by one forty-five." She pressed a key into Isobel's palm. "Keep this safe and lock up when you leave."

Isobel didn't know what to think. So she didn't. She rinsed brushes and stacked them to dry, and then packed away paints. She took the unused brushes to the cupboard next to the back window.

Glancing out, her heart double-thumped. She could see the hospital staff parking lot clearly from her second-story vantage point, and there was no mistaking that red-haired bulldog walking to his car. She hid behind the cupboard feeling silly.

He would never be able to see her from down there, but she wasn't taking any chances. If she did stay and take this job, it would require superhero skills to avoid that man.

7

Two weeks passed, and Isobel hadn't gotten around to fetching empty boxes. Some days she'd jot it down on her to-do list, but it was more out of habit than true intention. Every day now, she found herself at The Artist's Loft taking on more of the craft classes that drew in people of every shape and size. She could feel her confidence growing with each passing day.

Constant interaction with people left her drained and exhausted for the first week, but by the second week, her energy levels seemed to recover. The classes were never boring as she tackled some things she'd never even thought of doing.

At the end of each day, Rochelle would brief her on the next day's classes, tuck a few books in her hands, and send her home to prepare. That took care of her evenings, too.

Evenings at The Loft were Rochelle's sacred dominion. That was when the true artists came out and launched themselves into the deep: learning the skills of true art, not paddling in the shallows of crafts.

Part of Isobel longed to be included in that tightly knit group, yet she'd felt no hint of invitation from Rochelle and had not enough guts to ask for one.

But it was Friday night, and she was grateful that tomorrow was free. She glanced briefly through the book on candle making that she needed to absorb by Monday, but her brain rebelled and she tossed it on the side table. The weariness in her limbs led her upstairs to her bed, instead.

Many things had changed since she'd started working again, particularly her vampire-like sleep patterns. To her delight, she found herself sleeping through the night and waking up to sheets that were barely creased. Everything felt better.

She pulled on her soft pink satin pj's and wriggled beneath the duvet. On impulse, she leaned over and switched off her alarm clock. "I am going to sleep until I'm finished, and you"—she frowned at the clock—"are not going to stop me. So there!" She flicked the off switch on her lamp to end the conversation.

Talking to the objects in her house was one thing. Frowning and lecturing them? That just took on a whole new level of crazy. But as she lay back in the dark, soothing silence settling like downy feathers, she didn't care. About being crazy, about her missing muse... none of it mattered anymore. She was content.

Sleep kissed her eyelids and she drifted off.

****

A sound filtered through her consciousness to her dreams. Woodpeckers dancing endless circles around holey trees. Men driving powerful jackhammers, cracking up entire pavements before moving on. Her mom knocking on her door, yelling in her don't-be-late-voice, "Honey! It's time for school! Get up!"

She shot up in bed, dazed images crashing around her bed like breaking glass before vanishing in the light of her dawning awareness.

Bang bang bang! The sound was coming from downstairs, persistent knocking on the door.

Sleep clung like a thick fog to her brain. She stumbled out of bed, didn't think to throw on a gown, and clung to the balustrade to stop from falling. As she reached out to the handle, the banging started again.

Bang bang bang!

She jumped in fright. "I'm *here*! Stop banging..."

Liam Brigham stood on the porch, a blanket-wrapped bundle in his arms. He pushed past her the moment she opened the door and bumped the door shut behind him with his rear.

She reached up to put on the light.

"No, leave it off." His voice was sharp and he peered through the spyhole to check the street.

She squinted at the clock, the time just visible in the moonlight. "Two AM. Are you completely mad?"

"Bel, we're out of options and out of time."

"We? What are you talking about? There is no *we*. What are you doing here?"

"Here." He handed over the bundle in the blanket.

A corner fell, she saw the tiny sleeping face and it clicked. "No—"

Liam held a finger to her lips, "Just listen—"

"No! You are not doing this to me!"

"Trust me when I say right now you are this little girl's only hope." Liam's voice was a low whisper. "There isn't time to explain. Keep her here. Please, Bel." The look on his face told of twenty thoughts all crashing through his mind at once. None of them made it out his mouth. Instead, he exhaled sharply, gave her arm a brief squeeze, kissed sleeping Mia on the forehead, and let himself out.

"Oh God, what now?" she prayed. In an instant, Isobel was wide awake.

Mia stirred and moaned in her sleep.

Isobel's arms protested against the dead weight. Not knowing what to do, she climbed the stairs to her room and tucked Mia into her bed. Her tiny body looked lost in a sea of duvet.

Isobel was at a complete loss. It didn't feel right climbing into bed next to her, and it would be wrong to go sleep on the couch downstairs and leave her alone.

There was only one other option. She pulled the spare blanket off the end of her bed and propped herself up in the armchair in the corner with the blanket tucked under her chin. She watched the rise and fall of Mia's chest for the longest time.

Thoughts scrambled through Isobel, like looters in a riot. None of them logical, not one stopped long enough to be considered. Just endless churning in her head and a cold knot in her stomach.

This could not be happening.

At some point, sleep settled thickly on her lids.

8

A loud wail tore through the bedroom.

Isobel shot up and fell off the chair. Her bum hitting the carpet woke her. She shook her head to clear it and winced as pain lanced down her neck and through her shoulder. Nothing like sleeping upright in a chair to give one a crick in the neck.

In the middle of the bed sat the source of the wailing. Enormous tears trailed down Mia's cheeks. Red in the face from the effort of crying, she was inconsolable.

Isobel kneaded her neck and groaned. "So I guess you weren't part of some awful dream then..." Isobel did the only thing that made any sense. She panicked.

She picked Mia up and ran down the stairs as quickly as she could without dropping her. She fumbled with the front door lock and managed to get it open on the third try, using one hand only. She ran down the path with her siren baby going full blast.

Melindi would know what to do.

Her hand reached for the gate latch and she froze. How was she going to explain this? She turned back. Maybe water would work. She ran to the kitchen and turned on the tap.

Mia's back arched. She bellowed afresh and pushed away from the sink with both feet, toppling Isobel off balance.

She stumbled backwards, only just managing to

keep the thrashing toddler in her arms. Still, Isobel's back rammed into the counter, knocking her wind out and sending a bowl of fruit flying.

Mia stopped crying.

Isobel eased the child down in between gasps. She felt small hands lose grip of her leg as she clung to a barstool, willing the stars away and concentrating on sucking in each breath. It took a full minute to breathe normally again. As the blackness receded from her eyes, she heard silence.

No noise, no crying. Almost too scared to look, she peeped over her shoulder.

Mia was sitting in the middle of the kitchen floor. She had a squished banana in one hand and was smearing pulverised blobs of the sweet fruit into her mouth with the other.

Isobel sank to floor, sliding down the wooden knobbles of the barstool leg.

Mia finished the banana, dropped the peel on the tiles next to her, and held out her hand. "Taa!"

Isobel felt around for another magic, baby-silencing fruit, pulled the skin back, and held it out. Her heart was thumping in her ears.

Mia bum-shuffled forwards and took it out of Isobel's hand.

Their gazes caught for a moment, but the banana won, and Mia focussed her full attention on getting as much of it into her mouth as she could. Her sunburned skin had turned to flakes across her forehead and nose, all down her arms. If humans shed their skin like snakes, it would look like Mia.

Isobel's stomach twisted. "Slowly, baby. Don't choke."

Mia gagged as the banana pushed too far. She

pulled it out and resorted to squishing. No more made it to her mouth.

To Isobel's horror, Mia seemed intent on massaging the entire banana into the kitchen tiles. *I can't do this.* Isobel pushed herself off the floor, her eyes fixed on the living mess in the middle of her tidy life. She backed towards the fridge, pulled Liam's business card out from under a grinning duck magnet, and then turned and ran from the kitchen.

The little girl started crying. Heartbroken, gulping sobs.

Isobel's pulse raced. Her instincts warred within her—mostly she wanted to dive through the open lounge window and run as far and as hard as she could. Leave everything and get away. Yet she couldn't ignore the tiniest sliver inside urging her to go back into the kitchen and make it all better.

She did neither. Picking up the handset, she forced her trembling fingers to punch in Liam's number. Straight to voicemail. *No!*

She tried again. Still no answer.

The crying in the kitchen was getting louder.

She slammed the phone down, sank to the floor, and cried. Hugging her legs to her chest, she allowed hot tears of frustration to burn down her cheeks. *This can't be happening.*

It felt like an eternity as she huddled on the floor, frustration and desperation taking turns to punch her in the belly. Somewhere in her storm of tears, without her realizing, quiet had settled over the place. The softest touch on her arm made her look up.

Mia had found her. She stood quiet, her sun-ravished skin wet with tears of her own. Stormy grey eyes regarded Isobel with fierce thoughts, thoughts too painful for one so small to form into words. Her arms slipped around Isobel's neck and the child wriggled onto her lap.

Isobel froze. Banana assaulted her senses, slimy hands on her skin, sickly sweet stench clawed its way up her nostrils. She forced herself to breathe, to stay put.

Mia snuggled closer, the warmth of her body pressed tightly to Isobel. Warmth that soaked into her, intent on worming its way to her heart. The tiny blonde head tucked under her chin. Isobel felt every muscle in Mia relax as she shuddered out a breath, the raggedness that followed too many tears.

Isobel froze. She was stuck. It would be easy to surrender, to allow this little girl in. Yet opening that door would let other things out. Things she wasn't ready to look at. Her arms stayed glued to her sides. Folding them around this life would be to sign acceptance on the dotted line.

****

"Doctor, can I adjust this drip?"

"Go ahead." Liam felt the buzz of the phone in his pocket. He ignored it and finished writing out a script. "Good news, Mrs. Morwana. You'll be going home today." He handed her file to the nurse. "Make arrangements?"

The elderly lady in the hospital bed clapped in delight.

Liam's phone buzzed again. "Excuse me, will you? Sister Taylor will help you." He moved into the passage and checked the bright screen. Isobel, her second call. His finger hovered over the answer button, but he changed his mind and put the phone back in his pocket. It was too soon. It was time to do his paediatric rounds, anyway. She would have to wait.

Tanisha was a slight, three-year-old asthmatic who had come in during the night fighting for each breath. She was sleeping now, stable, though still weak. Nine-year-old Vaughn was in the bed next to hers, recovering from a severe allergic reaction to an antibiotic that he'd been given for bronchitis.

Liam moved through the ward, each little face brightened as he came close, sharing a joke here, a whisper of encouragement there.

Tanisha's mom was waiting for him in the hall, "Doctor Brigham, thank you for rescuing my little girl. I don't know what I would've done if..."

He stopped her with a hand on her arm. "Don't go there. You don't need to, she'll be just fine."

"You're right. Honestly, your life is a gift from God to us. If you had a horse and some shiny armour, you would be our knight!"

He laughed, "Well then I'd better be on my way, there are some dragons that need slaying. I'll be back later to check on her."

As he walked the familiar passages, his thoughts turned toward Mia and Isobel. Deep in his gut lurked a certainty that Mia's mom was no longer alive. There was something going on in this town that was not right. Two apparent suicides, two children swallowed up into the welfare system without a trace...

He wanted to punch something. Better yet, some*one*. In all the uncertainty, he knew two things— Mia needed someone and so did Isobel. It made perfect sense that they should be together.

Everybody needs somebody.

A dull ache stirred at the thought, but he shut it off and checked his watch. Time to get to his rooms.

9

Melindi answered the doorbell looking as if she'd had a spectacular fight with her duvet and lost. She grinned when she saw Isobel. "Hey! Come in. Just don't mind the mess." Then she saw the small person on Isobel's hip. "And who is this?" Her eyebrows would have formed question marks if they could. "Come inside. You can introduce us over some tea."

Mia stretched her arms to Melindi and giggled.

Isobel was taken aback. It was the first time she'd heard Mia laugh.

Melindi reached out and took her.

"Look at you! Come here."

Mia fell into her arms, still covered in banana.

"Oh, you have been busy, haven't you? My little banana girl."

Mia responded to her cooing with a dimpled smile.

Melindi's warmth washed over Isobel, who stood rooted to the welcome mat. A twinge of something green tiptoed across the back of her mind. Jealousy? How strange. She frowned as Melindi tugged her inside. Isobel narrowly avoided tripping over the train set that sprawled the entire length of the entrance hall.

Gunfire echoed through the house, but Melindi rolled her eyes. They found Ben in the lounge, his face lit blue from the TV. "Ben! Put it off! You are too young to watch that police show. How many times must I tell you?"

"But, Ma, you must see this gadget they've got. It shows blood stains even after they've been washed off!" He hovered protectively over the power switch, eyes flitting between the action on the screen and his mom's finger of doom. *Please* was etched into every contorted muscle of his face.

"Ben, it's not the gadgets that I have an issue with."

"It's not that bad. Watch and see." The words had barely left his lips when the actor in the cream suit doubled over, blood splattering across his lady friend, who erupted in a scream that could curdle chocolate milk. Ben flicked the switch, hid the remote behind his back, and grinned at his mom.

Melindi said nothing. She didn't have to. "Find some building bricks, boy. Play something that doesn't involve bleeding, OK?"

The boy looked dismayed.

Isobel stifled a snort.

Melindi rolled her eyes and then made sure her back was to Ben before catching Isobel's eye with a smile and a wink. "Come, neighbour, let's get this little mess cleaned up."

They climbed the stairs, stepped over a neatly parked collection of cars and a three-legged dinosaur cast in the role of a popular movie's giant monster.

"I'm going to run a bath for this sticky miss. Is that OK?" Melindi didn't wait for an answer, but led Isobel to a tiny bathroom. Soon the bath was bobbing with floating ducks and bubbles. She undressed Mia and popped her in the tub. The child laughed as she nearly disappeared under the thick, white foam.

"Tea?"

"Please." Isobel felt a moment of panic as Melindi left.

Mia swatted bubbles happily.

What am I going to do? This child needs her own mom. Not me. Anyone but me. Her thoughts went no further.

Melindi came back and put a steaming cup in her hands.

Isobel sat on the toilet seat, took a sip, and felt lost

Melindi plopped herself on the plastic kiddie step. "Jacques is away, again. Lilly is napping. What's going on in your life?"

Isobel's gaze strayed to Mia who was blowing holes in the bubbles and clapping them between her hands. Tendrils of blonde hair stuck to her face in the steam. The question hung thick in the air, unasked, but demanding an answer.

"She is...her mom is going through a difficult patch and I need to look after her. For a while." Isobel cleared her throat and studied the flowers on her cup. The whole truth was something Isobel couldn't make sense of.

"How long will she be with you?"

Isobel shook her head. She put down her cup and frustration overwhelmed her. "No idea. Who am I kidding? I don't know the first thing about kids! What am I going to do? I'm not ready for this. I never will be."

"I felt like that when Ben was born. Don't worry, Bel. It's in you. Be gentle on yourself. It will take time." Melindi put down her tea, took a bottle of baby shampoo, and poured a little into her palm. She began massaging the bubbly shampoo into Mia's hair. "You're a quiet little thing, aren't you?" Melindi rinsed out the suds and gestured to Isobel to pass conditioner.

"She really doesn't say much, does she? How old is she?"

Isobel cringed. "Two-ish."

"I would have guessed that. OK. This is how kids work. They need food—three small meals a day and some fruit and water in between. Avoid sugar as much as possible." She grinned at Isobel. "My kids zoom on sugar. It's terrifying. Other than that, they need a regular bedtime and a nap in the afternoon. Most of all? They need love. Lots and lots of love. Just like us, really. It's how we're built."

"You make it sound simple."

"It is, actually. She's a person like you, just... small." She rinsed and conditioned Mia's hair, took her out of the bath, and wrapped her in a fluffy pink towel. A layer of Mia's peeling skin came off on the towel as Melindi patted her dry. "This sunburn is bad. Do you have cream?"

Tears welled in Isobel's eyes. She didn't trust herself to speak, just shook her head.

Melindi caught the undercurrent. "Do you have anything for her? Clothes?"

Isobel shook her head at each question. She bit her tongue to stop the tears. The pain made it worse and one tear escaped down her cheek.

A loud wail from the nursery echoed through the house.

"Lilly. I'd better go get her. Here." She handed Isobel a mismatched wad of boy's clothes and a diaper. "Dress her in these."

Isobel took the pile, eyed the silent little girl who studied her with serious eyes, and wanted to run.

****

The sun was setting as Isobel and Mia walked home.

Ben hopped and skipped along with them, carrying a bag full of useful things from his mom. He dumped it on the kitchen floor, wrinkling his nose at the dried banana mess still plastered all over the tiles. He hugged Isobel's knees and his cast caught on the back of her pants. "Whoops! Sorry!"

She tousled his hair with a grin.

"Thank you for helping us home, Ben. Off you go. We don't want your mom to worry."

He waved and ran down the path, clanging his splinted arm on the gate on the way out. That boy had one speed, full tilt.

Isobel's arms ached from carrying Mia, who was rubbing her eyes and yawning. Isobel had spent the day watching Melindi mother her own two and effortlessly expand her love to include Mia as well. She had fed, corrected, and laughed with them. Love flowed from the gentleness of making an 'owie' better to the fierce sternness that kept tiny fingers from electrical sockets.

Being around her for the day had shifted something inside Isobel. She felt a twinge of confidence and the slightest stirring of something else she couldn't identify.

The stairs creaked under their combined weight.

"I think we should go shopping for you tomorrow, Mia. You can't live in boys' clothes."

Mia didn't answer, but lay her head on Isobel's shoulder. By the time they reached the top of the stairs, she was asleep.

Too worn out to think, Isobel tucked her into the big double bed and crawled in next to her. Half the night sleeping upright in an armchair has a way of tiring one out. Somewhere in the middle of her second yawn, Bel blacked out.

****

Liam checked his watch. The day's rounds were over, and he was off duty until morning. By the time he locked the door to his rooms, he had made up his mind. He had been itching all day to see how Isobel and Mia were getting on. It wouldn't hurt to stop by on his way home.

Between him and his car, a street kid sat waiting. In spite of the heat, he wore a holey jersey which hung on his sharp shoulders as if off a coat hanger. Leaning on the lamppost, more bones than flesh, his face lit up when he saw Liam. "Money for bread, *baas*?"

Liam grinned and shook his head. He couldn't solve South Africa's street-kid problem, but this one boy had crept into his heart.

"You know I don't give you money. Here, take this." He took his untouched lunch—peanut butter on whole wheat, a green apple the size of his fist, and a bottle of grape juice and handed it over.

The boy took his prize, a flash of white teeth Liam's only thanks, and skittered off to find a safe place to eat.

Liam eased into his vehicle and pulled out of the parking into the stream of traffic.

Sunset washed the sky in an orange glow. A breeze played with the palms lining the street.

In the rear view mirror, he caught sight of a red pickup pulling out. Home time was in full swing— even for such a sleepy holiday town. Liam indicated left, turning off the main road towards the suburbs.

Two cars behind him, the pickup did the same.

Liam frowned. He shook his head at the paranoia. All the unknowns were obviously getting to him. To prove to himself that he was being an idiot, he began weaving through the suburb in a random pattern of lefts and rights. He checked his rear view.

Whoever was in the Ford was determined to stay on his tail.

Fear and frustration shot through Liam. Bel and Mia were in trouble, and he was the cause. Every male instinct in him shouted *defend, protect, and make right*. Yet cold reality said otherwise. The only way to keep them safe was to back off completely. He dare not lead whoever was following him to their home. He checked his phone: eight missed calls throughout the day. *Oh, Bel. I can only hope that one day you will understand.*

He turned the car away from her street and drove toward home with a heart of lead.

10

Déjà vu slapped Isobel awake.

Mia's heartbroken howl tore through her eardrums with the same bone rattling intensity as a jet taking off in the back yard.

This time, Isobel knew exactly what to do. She'd postpone her panic until after offering Mia a banana. She carried the child downstairs, popped her on the floor on a clean towel, and put a peeled fruit in her hands.

Mia's cries dried up instantly as she busied herself breaking off chunks and getting them into her mouth.

Isobel's body was moving, but her brain was still deeply entrenched in her pillows. She went through the motions putting the kettle on and cleaning yesterday's banana from the tiles. By the time her floor shone and her second cup of tea was in, she felt ready to face this tiny creature who had thrown her life into chaos.

Isobel rang Liam's mobile again, not expecting him to answer. He didn't. *Big surprise.* She took a banana for herself, pulled back the peel, and on impulse sat on the floor next to Mia.

Mia stopped eating, studied the banana in Isobel's hand and looked at her own. She turned back to Isobel and grinned.

Isobel thought her heart might pop. Then it hit her. "You have teeth. We haven't brushed them for days.

What was the good doctor thinking trusting me with you?" She groaned. Just when she thought she was getting the hang of this.

Mia, on the other hand, was superbly unconcerned about dental hygiene. She found it far more interesting to squish the last bit of banana into the towel.

****

Isobel felt like a pimple on a prom date as she walked into the shop holding hands with a two-year-old dressed in oversized boy clothes.

Mia was barefoot and did not want to be carried. She communicated the fact in the car park very clearly, even though she'd not spoken a single word.

Isobel wasn't up to fighting and decided to let her walk. Nobody died from cold feet. Or embarrassment either, for that matter.

The next few hours felt like something Isobel had borrowed from someone else's life. She bought a pink dinosaur toothbrush and bubblegum flavoured toothpaste. A packet of disposable diapers went into the trolley; she threw in some training panties and a potty too.

Mia sat in the trolley sucking on a lollipop, taking it all in her stride.

By the time Isobel got to the clothing section, she couldn't suppress the smile on her face. She picked out a few t-shirt and short sets covered in fairies, three summery dresses, a soft knitted sweater in swirls of turquoise and purple, and two polar fleece tracksuits for the cold snaps. "You are costing me lots of money, little girl. It's a good thing Rochelle has kept me so busy."

Rochelle! Tomorrow was Monday.

Isobel was supposed to be teaching that candle-making class. She paled at the thought of Mia running free in the studio. That would never work. Her only option was to ask Melindi. She cringed at the thought. Melindi had her hands full between her AWOL husband, baby, and Ben with his broken arm. It wasn't fair to add a toddler to that mix.

Isobel had no other choice.

****

The studio reeked of hot wax.

Kez-lyn waved her half-finished candle towards the bubbling pot and prodded Savannah in the ribs. "Give me your legs. I'll wax them while we're at it. Save you the trouble of shaving."

"No way! I'm not letting you anywhere near me. Look at what you're doing to your candle, and it isn't even finished yet."

Kez-lyn held up her work in progress. It was bent and looked rather sad. "What? It has character."

Savannah snorted. "That's a little more character than I want my legs to have, thank you very much!"

Even Maggie laughed.

"OK, everybody, this is your next step." Isobel sent a loving thought Melindi's way as she gathered her Monday morning ladies around her. Much to Isobel's relief, Melindi had agreed to watch Mia. The ladies were quiet for once as she demonstrated adding scent to the classic dipped candles they were working on. "It's that simple ladies. Once you've dipped them, you hang them up here to dry. Careful with this hot wax. I wouldn't recommend it for hair removal." She winked at Kez, who mock-rolled her eyes. "Once it is properly set, we'll melt and add the second colour. Any questions?"

"I do!" Maggie hardly ever spoke. When she did, everyone gave her their full attention. "Why are you looking so happy, Isobel? I haven't seen you this joyful since we met you."

Mischa nodded. "She's right, you know. You are looking radiant. Have you met somebody?" Her face had that nudge-nudge-wink-wink look written all over it.

"Gosh no! Ladies. No. It's not what you think."

"What is it then? Do tell…" Jules put her candle down.

They all put their candles down.

Bug. Microscope. Earth, eat me now.

"Seriously, ladies. I…just…really like making candles." She plastered a smile as bright as a plastic sunflower on her face. "Gosh, look at the time. We'd better carry on. Who wants pink next?"

The ladies shared a look, stuck stubborn hands on their hips, and pointedly ignored their candles.

Isobel squirmed.

Maggie softened first. "It's fine, Bel. You can tell us when you're ready. Right, girls?"

Isobel shot her a thank-you-I-owe-you look, and the candles took centre stage amidst a low muttering that included the phrases "getting off too lightly" and "spilling the beans."

****

Dr. Liam Brigham had spent more money in the hospital's coffee shop over the last four days by accident than he had in all the years of working there.

A Monday lunchtime consultation with one of the surgeons regarding a complicated appendectomy put him next to the window.

He looked out—a simple act that had nearly stopped his heart. In the window of a building across the road, he'd seen Isobel. At first, he thought he must be mistaken, but he kept watching.

She ran fingers through her hair, catching it together in a low ponytail.

And he knew it was Isobel. Every day since, he'd fought the urge to live at this window just to see her. To know that she was OK. He kept hoping for a glimpse of Mia. Since the beginning of the week, he had seen Isobel at least once a day. This was good.

But her missed calls had dried up three days ago. This was not so good. She'd given up on him.

He kept telling himself that this was all part of the plan.

Sometimes, she felt so close, he caught himself wanting to knock on the glass and wave. Logic always prevailed. So he stuck his hand in his pocket, bought coffee, and drank it while staring out the window, trying not to look suspicious.

11

Exhaustion had a firm arm around Isobel and seemed intent on being a loyal companion.

Mia was finally asleep upstairs.

Isobel frowned at the supper dishes that lay waiting for her in the kitchen. She ignored the two loads of unfolded laundry that were collecting creases and poured a glass of mango juice. She picked her way between the borrowed toys that littered the lounge floor and collapsed on a couch with a yawn. *How does Melindi do this? With two of her own and Mia?* She took a sip and set it aside. The smell brought back memories of the day she babysat Lilly. One afternoon had been too much for her, how was she going to cope indefinitely?

It had been four days since she'd asked Melindi to watch Mia while she taught. Mia was always happy when she fetched her, and Melindi seemed to be managing having an extra body to look after. This was by no means a long term solution, but then who knew how long she would even have Mia?

The phone rang and she forced herself off the couch to answer. It would wake Mia if she left it ringing, and getting her to sleep again would take more energy than getting off the couch.

"Bel, I need to come see you." Melindi's voice was thick with emotion.

"What's going on? Are you all right?" A chill shot

through Isobel. "Can I come to you?"

"No. The kids...mustn't hear. I'm coming."

"I'm here, just come—"

The line went dead.

Bel ran to unlock the door. She met her friend at the gate.

Melindi was a mess.

Sick fear twisted Bel's stomach. "Is it Ben? Lilly?"

Melindi shook her head.

Bel led her to the lounge.

Her friend squeezed deep into the corner of a couch, hugging a pillow to her chest. It took a long time for Melindi to calm down enough to be coherent. When she did, she sounded hollow, gutted. "I should have known. I'm such a fool. All these years, I've believed the best. I've trusted and ignored any suspicions. He is always away on business. I kept telling myself he was doing everything he could to provide for his family." She buried her face in her hands as the tears started again.

Bel reached for a tissue and tucked it into Melindi's hand.

"Your husband is..."

Melindi nodded. "I found emails. Dates, hotel names. It was all right there. He didn't even try and hide it. He must think I'm a halfwit. I know I'm not exactly a technology goddess, but I obviously know more than he thought." She blew her nose, "Now I really know more than he thought."

"Oh, Melindi. I don't know what to say. I'm so sorry. What are you going to do? Leave him?"

Melindi drew her feet up on the couch, hugging her knees. She shrugged. "I need to think it all through. Maybe I'll take the kids and visit my mom. In fact, I'm going home to pack. I don't know that I can be in that house alone one more night." As if someone shot electricity down her spine, she got to her feet and hugged Bel.

"You are doing the right thing, Melindi. Good for you."

Without another word, Melindi hugged her again and let herself out.

Bel sank onto the couch in shock. An avalanche of emotions dumped over her. Sadness for her friend's pain, happiness that she'd found new fire, panic at being left alone with Mia. That one screamed loudest of all. *I can't do Mia without Melindi. I can't.*

****

Lying in bed, Isobel heard the car leave.

True to her word, Melindi had packed up her kids and left at six in the morning.

Mia was stretched out like a starfish next to Isobel, taking up far more bed than a two-year-old should. Her breathing was deep and even.

Isobel rolled onto her side, facing the little girl. In the half-light of morning, she studied the child's face. The sunburn was gone. Melindi's cream had worked, leaving Mia's skin smooth and soft. It was a shade or two darker than what it would have been, but the angry red, the long flakes—all of that was over. *What am I going to do with you today, Mia?*

Her ladies were due in at 9 AM for their first session with acrylic paints. They didn't know it, but the pieces they were to work on would serve as auditions for the evening art class. The *real* art class. If a student's work showed promise, she would be getting a personal invitation from Rochelle herself.

Isobel thought of Mia and all those pots of paint and cringed. She felt a twinge about the art class too, something she would probably never be part of. *Whatever. It didn't really matter.*

Mia had changed so much in such a short time.

Bel still had moments of blind panic, but she and Mia were settling into a rhythm of life together that soothed a tender spot that was buried too deep for her to look at. She no longer thought about next year, or next week. Each day came with just enough energy and emotional strength to see her through to bedtime.

Sooner or later, Mia would have to go, and Bel had to keep the walls up or that day would be the end of her. That single thing took more energy than everything else combined.

She watched Mia's eyes flutter open as consciousness kissed away the last traces of sleep. Isobel braced herself, waiting for the wake-up scream.

Mia rolled onto her side. She saw Bel and a grin of thorough delight crept over her face. She crawled over and tried to stick a chubby finger up Isobel's nose.

Bel laughed, turning her head away.

As if determined to find out what she kept in there—such a tempting dark hole—Mia clambered on top of her, straddling her ribcage. She waited for Bel to look her way and tried again.

Choking through her laughter and the weight on her chest, Bel grabbed her hand and blew a raspberry in her palm.

Mia dissolved in a puddle of giggles. When her laughing fit subsided, she let out a single breath and stretched out on top of Bel, blonde head resting on her chest, arms draped either side. "Mine."

That single word sent a shockwave through Bel. Tears sprang unbidden to her eyes. No longer able to fight, her arms folded around the little girl. She hugged her close and felt her carefully constructed walls shatter.

12

Mia sat in the middle of the table, silently studying the faces cooing over her.

"Oh my gosh! Bel!" Mischa was smitten. "She is a living doll! Is she yours?"

"Yeah, you've been holding out on us!" Kez ran her fingers through Mia's silken hair. "You never told us about this."

Jules stared at her, head tilted sideways. "I wish I could trade one of my boys in for such a beautiful little thing."

"So you say." Savannah laughed. "You wouldn't trade your boys for anything!"

"You're right, Savs," Jules said. "Would be nice to have this hair to play with though. Imagine shopping for dresses. All I get to buy are shorts and tees." She smiled wistfully at Isobel. "Introduce us."

Isobel felt the knots in her shoulders twist tighter. "This is Mia. I'm looking after her for a while. I did have someone to keep her during the mornings, but it didn't work out. So here we are." She looked from face to face, trying to gauge their reaction to having their kid-free mornings invaded by a two-year-old.

Maggie rounded the table and snaked an arm around her waist. "So this is why you've been so happy? It all makes sense."

At that moment, Mia decided she'd had enough of being the zoo attraction. She stood and held her arms out to Isobel. "Mine!"

Isobel reached out her hands and the little girl jumped into them with complete trust and a gleeful laugh that provoked a fresh round of aahs.

Rochelle would have her head on a plate.

"Ladies, let's paint!"

****

"Doctor, why are you in such a foul mood?" Angie slapped a pile of patient folders onto Liam's desk with more force than her standard swat. She stood frowning at him, for once apparently not giving any thought to the patients lining the walls of the waiting room like wilted ferns.

Outside, the wind picked up, sandblasting the building in fitful gusts.

Concern for Isobel and Mia gnawed at him constantly. He barely slept at night. Given his current frame of mind, not answering seemed the best option. In fact, it was the only way to avoid swearing. Try as he might, he couldn't help frowning back at her.

She waved a frustrated hand at him. "You see! There you go again. What is going on? You'll lose patients with that attitude."

"I am losing patience right now!"

Angie gasped, her mouth working like a stranded goldfish.

Liam ran fingers through his hair. "I'm sorry. That was out of line." *I have to get out of here.* "There's been an accident and I need to go to the hospital immediately. Get hold of the doctor on call to come and see to this lot. I'll be back as soon as I can."

Angie was still recovering and he took full

advantage of the fact to leave. There was no accident, no broken bodies needing stitching, but somehow he felt like the casualty. For the first time in a very long time, he turned his heart toward Heaven.

Half an hour later, Liam Brigham stood at the coffee shop window, the steaming cup in his hand a ticket to catching a glimpse of where his heart seemed to live lately. He was a few swallows away from needing a refill when he thought his eyes must be playing a trick on him.

A tiny blonde flash streaked past the window across the road. Seconds behind, he saw Isobel. Relief turned his knees to jelly. They were alive and together. As he watched, they both ran past the window again, going the other direction. Isobel was trying to catch Mia and not managing. Whether it was fun or sheer naughtiness, he couldn't tell from this distance.

Thank You, Father. He'd asked in desperation earlier, pleaded with God to let him know that they were both alive, and here he'd seen them for himself. Relief flooded his being. *Now to face Angie and that waiting room full of sick people.*

****

It was only after all the ladies had left, that Isobel found the mess.

Mia had spent half the lesson digging though and unpacking the ladies' bags and trying to open cupboards. They had taken it all in stride, laughing at her antics, but Bel knew their painting had suffered because of her lack of attention and input.

For the last bit of the lesson, Mia had grown very quiet and, much to Bel's relief, managed to keep herself busy.

Isobel found Mia asleep around a corner, an open tub of blue paint clutched in her arms. Her hands were blue. Blue hand prints covered the walls in between smeary blue rainbows as high as her short arms could reach. The floor had received less of her attention, but still boasted its fair share of blue splatters.

I am so dead. This is not working.

****

Liam unlocked the door and dumped his bags in the hallway. He breathed deeply, slowly in and out, relieved that the day was over. Not in the mood for cooking, he put two slices of whole wheat in the toaster, threw some eggs in a pan, and ate an apple while they cooked. Living alone, he avoided the dining room table more often than not. He took his plate out to the deck instead. He loaded his fork and had it half way to his mouth when his phone beeped. *Later.*

He ate, rinsed his plate under the running tap, stacked it to dry, then went for a swim in the rectangular pool he'd had put in last summer. He'd chosen the shape because it was how he liked his life, predictable and practical. No weird curves or unnecessary shapes. He towelled himself dry and remembered the message that was waiting for him.

He pressed the button to open the text message.

I can't do this anymore. Mia is too much for me I will be taking her to the welfare office tomorrow. Isobel.

He exhaled sharply. Dropping Mia with Isobel had been a risky gamble from the start. She had managed far beyond his expectations, breeding a false sense of hope within him. He should have known better.

****

The 3AM jackhammer started again downstairs.

Isobel woke from a semi-doze, knowing exactly who was at the door. She'd slept in her clothes in expectation of this visit. Creeping from the room so as not to disturb Mia, she paused to zip her cardigan, and then ran down the stairs two at a time. She flung the door open.

Liam stopped just short of knocking on her forehead.

Isobel stepped back silently, and he made his way to the lounge. Remembering his first midnight visit, she ignored the light switch and drew the curtains in the lounge back instead. Moonlight flooded the room in soft blue light. Every instinct made her want to sit opposite him, but for the sake of quiet whispers, she joined him on the couch.

"Bel, please—"

She crossed her arms and watched him flounder.

"To give that little girl up is to give her life away. Believe me—"

"Believe you? Believe that you care about this little girl or her life? Who are you to decide what's best for her? She could have family out there. Surely the authorities—"

"Look, I am in touch with the authorities, at least the ones I can trust. But we need to leave Child Welfare out of it. Something is wrong in the system."

"Something will always be wrong in the system."

"No, it's more serious than that. I had to keep Mia safe."

"Right. So you dumped her off with a total

stranger."

"Look, I know it was a lot to ask. I know that she came out of nowhere and has turned your life inside out—"

"Why me?"

"Don't you think for a moment that there was something—Someone—leading you to that beach in the first place? Is there no sense in you that you've been hand-picked for this, Bel?" He reached for her hand, but Isobel pulled away.

"And you think it's fair to dump her on me and disappear? No support, no help. Liam! You won't even answer when I phone you! I can't do this alone."

He wiped a hand down his face and exhaled sharply. "I know. It isn't fair of me to—"

"No! It isn't! I don't know what you were thinking!"

He stood up and paced.

"Liam, talk to me. You hint at things, but you won't tell me what's really going on. I cannot live in this limbo. How do I build a life around this little girl"— her voice broke as tears came—"only to have her snatched away from me days, weeks, or months from now? I'm not that strong."

He sank to his knees, hands on hers. "I don't know what is going on. All I have are suspicions and a gut that says things are wrong." His shoulders slumped. "Please don't give her up. I just need more time."

It was time to come clean. She sat back, stubborn arms firmly crossed. "I've no intention of giving Mia up." It was barely more than a whispered breath.

"What?"

"I can't."

"You nearly killed me."

"Oh, rubbish. You're a big boy."

"No, Bel. That was low."

"And you don't think your dump-and-run was?" This man was unbelievably thick.

He flopped on the couch as if his muscles had left for Hawaii. His expression showed that his brain was scuttling in twenty directions.

"Well, that's good. I am seriously happy. Oh grief, Bel! So the text you sent...?"

"Sneaky plot. You wouldn't have come otherwise."

He stared at her, speechless

She'd never seen him at a loss for words before. It made her want to giggle.

"You honestly think I didn't want to come? You have no idea what we're dealing with."

"Well, of course not. You won't talk to me!" From wanting to giggle, to wanting to slap in less than a millisecond. This man was infuriating.

"I couldn't come. Someone is following me. They know I have a connection to Mia. Bel, they want her."

"Who? What are you talking about?"

"Like I said before, she isn't the first. Parents disappear. Kids are taken and placed without a trace. Something is wrong. Very wrong." He put an arm around her shoulders hugging her close. "But you aren't giving her up. I can't tell you how happy that makes me."

She picked up his arm, dumped it back on his lap and moved to the end of the couch. As far away as she could. *Heart, stop it!* "Great. What now? Here's the thing, you see conspiracy theories. What if you're wrong? What if they're just unconnected tragedies. What if Mia has a family out there looking for her? I owe it to her to find out." Bel took a moment to find courage. "Liam, I can't live not knowing. She is invading my heart whether I like it or not. We need to get her back to her family now, or I might not survive it when the day comes that she has to leave. Let me help you find out what's going on. What have we got to lose?"

He was shaking his head before the words had left her lips. "What have we got to lose? You don't get it, do you? Whoever these people are, they are not scared to kill. You are not getting involved."

"Excuse me? Just how far are you with your investigations? How has ignoring us helped you? Hmm? Progress?"

He glared at her.

"I take it not very far."

He knuckled his forehead and groaned. There was nothing to say.

13

Bel waited for the sun to peep through her kitchen windows before phoning Rochelle.

Liam was still tucked under a blanket on her couch downstairs, the door at the top of the stairs locked to satisfy her insides.

The first thing she had to do was quit her job with Rochelle.

If Liam's instincts were right, Mia wouldn't be safe at a playschool, and taking her to class didn't work.

She braced herself and dialled.

"You'd better have a good reason for phoning so early."

"Rochelle, I do. I need to come see you."

"Well, that's good because I need to see you, too. Meet me at the studio in half an hour."

Isobel's heart sank. Tiny blue handprints flashed in her mind. She had scrubbed off every last trace, but Rochelle must have found out. *Well, I won't be going back anyway, so getting fired doesn't really matter.* Knowing that, though, didn't stop the stab of regret.

She woke Liam with coffee. He was a sleepy mess—dark-ringed eyes, hair a flaming muddle in every direction. She shoved away the impulse to hug him. They'd agreed that he would watch Mia so that she could meet with Rochelle.

"Here is her banana. If you get that in, everything else should be fine. I'll be back as soon as I'm done."

He peered at her through one half-opened eye, stretched with a yawn.

She couldn't help laughing. "Are you sure you're up to this?"

He took the fruit and fell back on the couch, banana clutched on his chest like a bouquet in the hand of a corpse. He mumbled something unintelligible and waved her off.

"OK then. Have fun."

More mumbles.

She shook her head and left.

Rochelle was waiting for her as the lift opened.

Isobel felt like a school girl who'd been caught cheating on a test.

"You're here. Good."

"I want to apo—"

Rochelle's hand went up. "No, no. Allow me. I know what has been going on here."

"I can expl—"

A single arched eyebrow evaporated Isobel's words. She closed her mouth and braced herself for the tongue lashing.

"You, young lady, have single-handedly taken a bunch of woman whose collective talent didn't amount to much, and brought some true art out of them." Her fingers traced Kez-Lyn's once-beheaded fairy and she nodded with approval. "You are doing good work, Isobel. I want you to join my evening class."

What? Isobel stared as if Rochelle were speaking Russian. "So this isn't about blue paint?"

"Dear girl, sometimes you make no sense at all. Tonight's group has been together for a while, but I think it's where you need to be. Seven PM. Just bring yourself and a mirror."

Isobel thought her chest might pop. This was nothing short of a dream landing in her lap.

"I'll be taking today's classes. Rest today and I'll see you at seven."

Isobel walked right past the de-blued bit of room and felt the heat in her face. The quicker she left, the better. The lift button glowed as she pushed it. It seemed to be the only real thing in the room as everything else turned fuzzy, dreamlike.

There was no doubt in her mind that Rochelle's class would shatter the awful blank canvas drought. Isobel's dream was alive and it was coming for her. After years of chasing, beating life into something so dead it refused to quiver... it had sought her out. It had come to find her.

The lift was halfway to the ground floor when reality crashed in, rolling on the floor, laughing at her. She was halfway to her car when she realized she hadn't resigned. With a groan, she thumped her forehead into her fist. There was no way she could go back now.

Besides, Liam surely needed her.

Mia would be up and yelling by now.

What a mess.

****

Isobel turned her key in the front door expecting to hear chaos. Instead, the sounds of giggling filtered through the fresh morning air. She followed the laughter to the lounge. There she found Liam, still on the couch.

Mia had joined him.

He had one arm around her and was walking

teddy bear fingers on her palm with his free hand. Each step his finger-teddy took brought another delighted chuckle from the little blonde girl.

They looked up as she walked in.

Liam flipped the corner of the duvet back. "Come join us. There's plenty room."

Mia poked a finger in his chest and announced, "Mine." Her face dimpled into a grin at Liam.

It was too much for Bel.

She fled upstairs, locked herself in the bathroom. Jealousy and anger played a murky game of tag inside. None of what she felt made sense, but that just made it all seem worse. She sank to the floor with her head between her knees.

A few minutes later, Liam knocked on the door. "Bel, let me in."

"Go away." She hugged her knees and buried her face in her arms.

He slid down next to her.

She was too shocked to keep crying. "How on earth?"

He had the decency to look sheepish as he held up a mauled wire coat hanger, a thin plastic cutting board from the kitchen and the bathroom key.

"You are incorrigible!"

"If I knew what that meant, I might agree with you."

"Impossible. Awkward. Persistent. Actually — you're a bully. A plain, straight bully. Where is Mia?"

"Downstairs. She's fine. I gave her some things to play with. So what's wrong?"

"Nothing. My life is perfect."

"Bel, you are too old to sulk. Seriously."

Bel shuffled closer to toilet, determined to expand

the space between them. She bumped her head on the loo and he laughed. Laughed! "What is wrong with you? You are the most irritating person I have ever met. Ever."

He shrugged. "Probably. But I'm not here to talk about me. What's going on?" His voice soothed her. He'd be great around skittish race horses.

"I'm not a horse, do you hear me? So don't think you can mesmerize me with all that charm."

"What? What are you talking about?" His nose wrinkled as if he'd stepped in dog-doo. "You've lost me." He actually looked apologetic.

And you are messing with my sanity. "Never mind. None of it matters."

"Talk to me, Bel."

There was a tone to his voice that picked the lock on her heart as easily as he had the bathroom door. Her words rushed out before she could stop them. "Rochelle has invited me to art class." She closed her eyes to stop the tears, but they squeezed out anyway.

"That's great, right?" He was still floundering.

She gave him ten out of ten for not giving up. "It would be if I could go."

"Why can't you?"

Do you actually have a brain? "Uh, Mia? Remember? Little blonde girl downstairs?"

He held up his hands. "OK, listen. I've been thinking. First, when is your class?"

"Tonight at seven."

"That's good. This is what we're going to do. You are going to your class tonight. I am going to take a few days off. I'll watch Mia for you. When you come home, we can make some plans. How's that?" He was grinning as if he'd just solved the epic problem of world hunger.

****

A wave of nausea washed through her as she stared at the blank canvas in front of her. She was next to the window on the right of the class, second from the back.

Noise from the street below filtered up through the window. A fruit seller called out—peddling off her last few *naartjies*, a minibus taxi driver yelling over the thump-thump music playing from his van, recruiting passengers in the hopes of a full load. Real lives, tough lives.

She let it all wash over her, bringing her to the reality of the moment. Pencil on canvas? Not a real problem. Surely.

The sun was setting, washing her stark canvas in soft orange light. She couldn't help feeling intimidated as she glanced around the room at the other twenty artists. There was none of the playful banter that marked her morning class, none of the camaraderie that she'd come to look forward to.

Each one was centred, focused, ready to create.

Isobel felt like a polar bear at a beach party.

Rochelle stepped out of the lift and did a quick headcount. There was no special attention or welcome for Isobel. She moved right ahead with the business of the night. "Right everyone. Set up your mirrors next to your canvas. This evening we will be producing two canvasses. You'll have an hour for each one. Yes?"

A quiet murmur of agreement hummed through the room.

"Your first piece will be a simple self-portrait, a

pencil sketch. Your one hour starts now."

There was no time to think, no time to fret. Isobel picked up her pencil, breathed deeply, and turned to her pale face in the mirror.

What seemed like twenty minutes later, Rochelle stopped them. "Your hour is up. Pencils down. Fifteen minute tea break and we'll start part two."

Her voice filtered through to Isobel like an alarm clock penetrating a bizarre dream in which her muse had returned.

Isobel shook herself back to reality, stepped back to see what she'd done. The hour had flown. Strangely, having a short time seemed to work for Bel—her self-portrait was complete. And it was good. Her proportions needed some work, but the lines, the shading—it was all there. It was clearly her face.

She made her way to the tea table in a daze. *I actually drew something.*

A short man with a grey beard grabbed her hand and shook it with gusto. The top of his bald head was perfectly in line with her shoulder. "The name's Harry Reid. Your first time?"

Isobel retrieved her hand from his clench and nodded. She reached for a cup and busied herself making tea. *I drew!* She wanted to laugh and hug someone.

Harry was standing so close that she bumped into him as she turned for the milk. His coffee slopped down the front of his shirt.

The hugging urge evaporated. "I'm so sorry!"

"No worries, this shirt is my paint shirt. You'd know that if you were a regular. What is your name, love?"

I would rather fall out of this window than tell you that.

She was saved from answering by a lanky redhead who introduced herself as Sybil.

More handshakes followed: Bethany with her close cropped raven hair, Padu—a tall Indian with a love for ink sketching. All the artists were more relaxed and clustered together, chatting. It was as if the entire room had breathed out a collective sigh of relief at achieving the halfway mark.

Isobel felt the knot in her belly loosen.

Rochelle was beckoning the artists back to their places.

Isobel put down her sipped tea and tried hard to stroll back to her place. This was exciting.

The briefest hint of a smile touched Rochelle's lips. "I've had a quick tour around the room during the break, and I am very happy with what I saw. I must mention our newcomer tonight. She has produced an excellent piece of work. Isobel, good girl."

Across the room, Coffee-slop-Harry's face twisted in a smirk and he shoved both his thumbs in the air.

Isobel thought how nice it would be to throw a cream-pie at that face. She wasn't about to let some troll ruin her breakthrough night, so she slam-dunked him out of her mind and focussed on the instructions Rochelle was giving.

"The second part is simple. Come and fetch a rock from this pile. Smash your mirror." She held up a stern finger. "No whining about bad luck. It doesn't exist. Repeat your self-portrait. Any questions?" She gave a split second before retracting the question and waving them to work.

Isobel fetched her rock. It was smooth and fitted in her palm as if it was part of her. Her first tap was too light; the mirror remained unbroken. The knot was back in her belly. She hit with more force a second time, sending cracks skittering through the glass. A piece fell out as she set it up next to her canvas.

She set to work more reluctantly this time. Each stroke of her pencil brought more of her shattered face to life on the canvas. Each jagged piece, a silent scream...

You're broken. You're broken.

She felt a tear and ignored it. Jagged slivers radiated from the centre point of impact. Hot tears ran freely. She kept drawing. At times, barely able to see, Isobel persisted. Cold resolution cracked the whip over emotion. Her left eye was in three shards, she drew it—exactly as she saw it. Her right eye was gone, fallen with the missing piece. *I can't do this.*

Her mutilated face stared back at her from the canvas.

The cracks formed another image. Superimposed on her likeness was a baby. Not Mia, a newborn.

She dropped her pencil and fled.

14

Liam was worried. Isobel's art class finished over an hour earlier, and she still wasn't home. She might have got chatting and lost track of the time, but the disquiet in his gut told another story.

Mia had gone to sleep without any trouble, and he'd spent the rest of the time talking to God. The faith-fire of his teen years had dwindled and died, but since the disappearances, he'd found himself turning regularly Heavenward for answers. Praying normally brought a flood of bizarre peace, but tonight was different. Every time he brought up the topic of Isobel, his insides buzzed as if they'd been zapped with a stun gun. *God, what do I do?*

He took the stairs two at a time. He cracked the door as quietly as he could.

Mia was stretched out diagonally across Isobel's double bed. She was not about to wake up. Not for anything.

Liam couldn't risk being recognised, so he threw on a cap and pulled it low, turned his jacket collar up and let himself out the front door without turning the lights on. He was halfway down the path when he heard to faintest squeak of a spring. The swing bench! It could be wind, or it could be Isobel.

He felt his way back through thick darkness. He became aware of muffled breathing and fumbled through mud and bushes. The bench was on the porch.

As he drew closer, he saw a vague shadowy form.

Isobel huddled in the corner of the swing with her knees drawn up. She stared off into the blackness.

The bench started swinging as he landed. She didn't acknowledge him, and he said nothing. It could have been seconds or hours that they sat in silence, silence broken only by the creaking of the bench and lovesick crickets. He would sit all night if he had to.

She pulled her knees closer, her voice low. "It just takes one. I didn't know that."

"What do you mean?"

She shrugged. "I've just been thinking. It just takes one. One awful thing. Everything else shatters. It can never be made whole again."

"I'm not following. Talk to me."

She looked at him then, as if she hadn't realized he'd been there all along.

"What happened, Bel? What's your one awful thing?"

Car lights sliced through the dark. A vehicle pulled up next door.

"Melindi! She's back!" Bel tripped in her hurry to get off the swing. She fell over Liam's legs and landed with her elbow in his chest, hard enough to knock the wind out of him. "Grief, are you OK?" She didn't hang around to make sure but bolted down the path like a kid chasing the ice-cream van.

****

Melindi's door was barely open when Bel got to her. As she stepped out, Bel threw her arms around her. "You're back! How are you? Where are the kids?"

"Shhh! Look."

Both kids were deep in Z-land.

Even by moonlight, Bel could see the new lines on Melindi's face. The mess with her husband had taken its toll on her.

"Sorry!" Bel whispered. "Can I help you carry anything in? Are you back to stay or just fetching stuff?"

"Grab this bag for me. For now, we're back."

Isobel hooked the bag on her shoulder and carried Lilly upstairs, marvelling at how light she was compared to Mia. She tucked the sleeping baby into the cot under a blanket covered in singing sheep and then brushed soft curls away from her face.

When Isobel returned to the kitchen, she could see just how tired Melindi looked under the harsh fluorescent light. A grey pallor had replaced the healthy blush Bel remembered. It took three trips to bring everything in from the car.

Melindi coached a sleepwalking Ben from the back seat all the way to his bed. She came back to the lounge and yawned.

Bel took it as an unintentional hint. "You need your bed. Maybe we can catch up tomorrow?"

"I'd like that, Bel."

Bel eased the back door shut, hoping Liam would have given up waiting and gone to bed. The tinkle of a spoon in a cup said otherwise.

Liam was in the kitchen stirring sugar into his coffee."You want some?"

"I think I'm going to find my bed."

"We were still talking. I want to hear...about art. How was it?"

She noticed his hesitation, but played dumb. Her insides were safely locked away once more. Revisiting it all was not doing any good. "It was interesting. I managed to draw." The joy bubble that had come back with Melindi, popped as her own broken face flashed through her mind. She craved the oblivion of sleep. To shut it all off, make it go away. "Goodnight, Liam."

"Wait!"

"Sleep well."

"Uh, Bel?"

She was halfway up the stairs, "What?!" *If he dared inquisition her…*

"Throw me some blankets?"

****

The lift to Rochelle's loft was beginning to feel like nasty déjà vu.

Isobel rolled her shoulders and stretched, trying to shake off the last clinging remnants of sleep.

Liam had woken her with coffee and orders to get moving.

Rochelle had phoned and was expecting her for a meeting at nine.

Icy wakefulness shot through her—Rochelle had spoken to Liam. Rochelle knew there was a man living in her house. She didn't know there was a locked door between them, so who knew what conclusions she'd draw. Bel groaned and would have hit her head on the doors, but they opened.

She found Rochelle around the corner, sitting in front of Bel's own easel from the night before. She was studying Isobel's portraits with no expression on her face. The pencil in her hand tapped nonstop in her palm.

Suddenly Bel's feet felt far too heavy. It took all

her effort to keep walking.

Rochelle patted the barstool next to her. "These are good."

"Thanks. It was…challenging."

"I'll admit you're the first to run."

Bel didn't know what to say to that, so she didn't say anything.

"Let me tell you what I see. You are gifted with many talents. Before—you saw life in the fullness of its beauty, and because of your gifting, you could capture those moments on canvas with such clarity that others could share in it too. That is a unique and rare thing."

"You said *before*. Before what?"

"Something traumatic hit your life with enough force to break you into a thousand tiny pieces. It broke you, Bel." With the pencil, she gestured to Bel's missing eye. "And it stole your ability to see."

She stood up and turned towards Bel's shattered face. She began sketching, adding to the drawing, "You think you are broken and there is no hope of ever being whole. I tell you now, being broken has not stolen your sight. It has increased it." The pencil tip darted over the canvas like a dragonfly on a pond. "You see, Bel, life is beautiful, and that beauty has value. But life is also fragile and difficult. Tragedy and pain are real."

Bel's missing eye was coming alive beneath her skilled fingers. "Once you've walked the road of suffering, been broken by the weight of that which you were never meant to bear—you realize, He has been carrying you all along."

Strong hands were taking shape around her face. "In His hands, being broken does not rob you of all value. In His hands, being broken allows His life inside of you to spill out, and bring His Life to everyone you meet."

The cracks that destroyed her face, were slowly transforming into blazing light beams. Light that shone and sparkled, stretching beyond the confines of the canvas. Rochelle leaned close to add the last few lines. She put down the pencil and stepped back with her arms crossed.

Bel stared. Her pencilled face, radiant—so bright and beautiful that the unmarred face of her first portrait paled in comparison.

"It's incredible."

"His ways are incredible. You, my dear, have a class to teach."

The lift pinged and the room filled with happy chatter.

15

By the time Isobel got home, Mia was fast asleep. She'd nodded off halfway through her lunch, and Liam had managed to carry her upstairs and tuck her in without waking her. He had an irritating way of handling her that Bel hadn't quite nailed yet. *Show off.*

"Are you feeling better than last night?" He sported a checked dish towel in one hand and a squeeze bottle of double-strength lemon dishwashing soap in the other. He wielded them as a knight would his sword and shield. If any dirty dragons happened to show up, they'd be in some serious trouble.

"I am."

"Good. That makes me happy."

She found herself mesmerised.

He picked up a dripping plate and started drying it. The plate seemed to shrink in his hands. He worked his way methodically through the stack on the drying rack.

Bel leaned back against the door frame and watched. "Liam, I need to tell you something."

He stopped washing and took a cloth to dry his hands. "Should we go sit in the lounge?"

"No, just keep washing. It will be easier that way."

To his credit, he didn't say a thing about how weird women were, but picked up the cloth and carried on. "I'm all ears."

She floundered, not sure if she really wanted to do

this. She thought about the last ten years, ten years of running. Hiding the past away as if it would magically dissipate like morning mist under the gaze of the sun. It hadn't; she knew that now. Instead, it had all gone sour in her belly. *Where to begin?*

"Last night in art class we drew a self-portrait. Two in fact. The first was easy—it was just my face in a mirror and I actually managed to draw. The second part was awful."

Liam had run out of dirty dishes and was now re-drying the dry ones to keep her talking.

She noticed, but couldn't bear the thought of looking him in the eye while unpacking her insides. She pretended not to see. "We had to break the mirror and redraw our portrait. It was like being slapped in the face over and over with my own brokenness. It took a single hit to shatter my image, and then I knew that's what happened to me. It was one event that broke everything about me. That's why I couldn't draw, couldn't move on."

Liam had put the cloth over his shoulder and turned to face her. He towered over her, and she breathed in his closeness. Part of her wanted to run. The rest of her wanted to lean into the strength of his chest. Never mind lean, collapsing would do just fine too.

"Tell me, Bel." His voice was barely a whisper.

"I was in art school ten years ago. My mentor was—"

The doorbell rang.

Isobel didn't know whether to laugh or cry.

"I'll get it. You hold that thought." Liam left her in the kitchen.

"No! Liam!" She ran after him. This could not be

happening. She got to the door to find him introducing himself to Melindi as Mia's doctor.

Her friend's gaze took in his shorts and bare feet, the soggy cloth over his shoulder. This would go down as the weirdest house call in the history of medical science.

Melindi must have drawn her own conclusions. She grinned broadly at Bel. "Sorry to bug you guys. I really need a favour."

Mia started crying upstairs and Liam excused himself to go see to her.

Melindi grabbed Bel's arm, whispering furiously, "What on earth, Bel? What a catch! I'm so happy for you!"

"It's not what you think, really."

"Well it should be. He's adorable!"

"No, trust me. He drives me nuts. I pity the poor woman who gets him."

Melindi was smiling and nodding with *oh right.* written all over her face.

"You needed a favour?"

"I do. I've been invited to a single moms' thing tonight. I was wondering if you could watch the kids? But no, I can see you are busy. It's fine. I'll go next week."

"So there's no hope then...you and your husband?"

Melindi shook her head. "It's been too long. He doesn't want to stay."

"I'm so sorry."

"Don't be. It is just the way things are."

Liam came downstairs.

Mia was snuggled into his neck, fuzzy from her nap.

"So, who are we babysitting?"

****

Isobel sat on the couch with her feet drawn up. The buttery smell of popcorn drifted through from the kitchen accompanied by Liam's torturous rendition of Old King Cole—the only nursery rhyme he could remember.

Ben was swatting a ball with his cast, taking turns to aim at Lilly and Mia. Lilly was besotted with Mia and watched her every move.

When Melindi had dropped them off, Mia had taken time to study Lilly and Ben with her serious eyes before trying to stick her finger up their noses. Lilly had taken it in her stride, blinking and then letting out an enormous sneeze. Ben had swatted her hand away and laughed. That laughter had sealed it for Mia. She'd made up her mind: they would be friends. Probably forever.

Ben rolled the ball and it bumped into Mia's foot.

She looked straight at Isobel and said, "Ball."

Isobel wasn't sure she'd heard right.

"Liam! Come hear this!"

He came through with a mouth full of popcorn. "Huh?"

"Listen. Ben, roll the ball at her again."

Ben rolled it too hard, and it shot past Mia.

She turned and pointed. "Ball."

Liam dropped to the floor next to her. "What's this, Mia?"

She ignored the ball and pointed at his nose. "Mine!"

Ben slapped the carpet and laughed so hard Lilly

started crying.

Liam picked up the tearful baby. "Mamma Bel, I think it's bedtime for these little people. What do you think?"

Bel was at a loss for words. Liam was in his element, surrounded by little people. The whiffs of popcorn in the air had home threaded through them. It felt like a dream, a dream she didn't want to wake up from.

Three stories and a tall glass of water later, quiet descended on the house.

Liam flopped down in the corner of the couch. It would have been the most natural thing in the world to shimmy in next to him and lay her head on his shoulder.

She sat in the far corner, drawing her knees up between them like a wall.

"Should I bring some dishes and a cloth?"

She swatted at his leg, and he caught her hand, laughing. The laughter faded and his voice sank to little more than a whisper. "Seriously Bel, it's time you got that stuff inside, out. You were telling me about your art mentor."

"There's not much to tell, really. I was young and naïve. He was compelling and brilliant. It took many months, but he was patient. Persistent. I fell for him. I fell hard. He took me in and taught me art. He told me that…making love was the ultimate key to releasing your emotions. That was the one thing that would take my artistry to the next level."

Liam's fists clenched.

There was no emotion in the words that left her lips. She spoke as a news reader would from a teleprompter. The emotions were buried, and that's where they were going to stay. "Idiot that I am, I believed him. I was not the first he had his way with. According to his plan, it was all working out beautifully." Her eyes lost focus as she confronted the Pandora's box that she'd been denying so long. "The baby wasn't something he'd factored in though. That's where his plan fell apart. I suppose he thought I was like the other girls, that I was prepared. I wasn't. He was my first."

Liam reached across to take her hand.

She pulled away sharply and scratched an itchy spot on her head that wasn't itchy at all. "I was scared when I found out that I was having his baby. It wasn't the way these things are meant to happen. But to be honest, I was also excited. From the moment I knew, I loved this little person growing inside of me. I was so besotted with him, I hoped the baby would tie us together in some real, tangible way. I thought we could be a family." She floundered now, unable to put words to the unspoken horror she'd lived through. Ravenous pain that she'd never spoken out loud for fear of feeding it.

In an instant, Liam shifted closer and put his arms around her shoulders.

She stiffened against his touch, but he didn't back off. He said nothing, but he held on. She closed her eyes and surrendered to the safety of his arms.

"I remember waking up in terrible pain. My baby was gone. Stolen from me. The last thing I remember was him saying we'd be going out to celebrate. He bought me a drink—fruit juice, not alcohol. He insisted on it. To me, it was his way of acknowledging the baby was real, a little life worth protecting. I was so happy. I was with the man I loved most, and we were having a baby together. Life felt complete."

"So what you're saying is that he drugged you and took you for an abortion?"

"He had connections with some people on the medical faculty. They offered the service to students. It was all very hush-hush."

Liam's arm around her was shaking.

"I didn't know how to handle it, so I left. As far as I know, he's still there, teaching. It's as if it never happened. Some days I wondered whether it was all just a very long nightmare. But every time I faced a blank canvas, I knew the truth. I would never be whole again."

Liam drew her closer into his arms, as if he could absorb her pain if he just squeezed hard enough. "Which is why we can't let anything happen to Mia."

She pushed herself away from him. "Stop it, Liam! Let it rest. Nobody is hunting for her. Nothing bad is going to happen. Why do you keep bringing it up?"

He sat silent, stewing.

"Why does this bother you so much anyway?"

He breathed out, and the fight drained from him. "It just does. I have no evidence for you other than what my heart says. There must be some sort of syndicate, a group to draw in single moms. From there...who knows? Isolate and brainwash them? It sounds far-fetched, but it's possible."

"Isolate and brainwash? Liam, listen to yourself. You are sprouting ideas straight from the plot of some low budget movie. Even if you're right, what do we do? You can't keep living on my couch. Have you thought about how weird this arrangement is? You've got to get back to your practice. It's one thing to feel something is out of whack, but quite another to turn life upside down for a whim—a feeling that might not even be real."

"All the leads I've followed have come back with nothing. But I know things aren't right. If anything happened to Mia…"

"There is something you're not telling me."

He pointedly ignored her accusation. The man was selectively deaf.

"I don't know where to go from here," he said.

By the lamplight, she could see determination set in his jaw.

"But I know Someone who does. Pray with me, Bel."

16

Melindi was singing as she hung up washing in the morning sun.

Isobel could hear her from the kitchen.

Melindi had collected her two late the night before, but hadn't said much about her evening out. In hindsight, she was probably trying to give Isobel and Liam time alone.

Isobel cringed, realizing how wrong her friend's assumptions were.

Melindi's lilting song filled the crisp morning air with a lightness that had little to do with the rays of the sun.

Why was she so happy? Isobel wanted to go see, but Mia had her legs in a vice grip.

"Joooos!"

"You want some juice?" Isobel marvelled at the change in Mia since Liam had been living on the couch.

The baby had discovered a deep well of words within her and wielded them with determination. She seemed intent on catching up for the weeks of silence.

Isobel poured apple juice into a sippy cup they'd inherited from Ben. It sported red cars with fat yellow tyres.

Mia clapped, took the juice, and then flopped down onto the kitchen floor, her nappy wedged between her skin and the chilly floor.

Isobel unlocked the back door, latching it as she

went out. "Hey, neighbour. You are very cheerful this morning!" She leaned on the jasmine that hung in thick, fragrant clusters over the wall. The air filled with the sweet scent.

Melindi pegged a pink baby bodysuit to the line, left her washing, and walked over to where Bel leaned over the wall. "I feel like a new person. Last night was amazing."

"Tell me."

"There were eight other moms there. The lady running the meeting got us all to talk about how we came to be single moms. Each person had a chance to share. It was so good to realize that I'm not alone. I really think this group will be a lifeline for me."

"That's great! I'm so happy for you. You really need a good group of friends right now, especially if they can relate to what you're going through." The silence from the house set off alarms in her head. "I'd better go see what Mia is up to." Isobel squeezed her friend's arm and turned to the house.

Melindi called after her. "And you know the best part? They say that I've qualified for free one-on-one counselling."

Bel froze. She turned back. "Say that again?"

"I know! Too good to be true, but it really is happening. I've wanted to see a counsellor or someone just to get perspective, but money won't allow it. Now, it has found me."

"With whom?"

"I don't know. It doesn't really matter. Apparently, they use all the latest techniques to help you get to grips with your emotions. Isn't that awesome? The most amazing thing is that I'm the newest in the group and I'm the only one that they've chosen. Incredible, hey?"

Cold ice shot down Bel's spine.

Melindi laughed and covered her mouth with her hand. "Oh, flip. Bel, I'm not supposed to tell anybody. Forget that I told you, OK?"

"Why would you need to keep it secret?"

"I suppose they don't want to be inundated. It is free, after all."

Melindi had just described Liam's bad movie plot: *Isolate and brainwash.*

It made Bel's belly twist. She shook her head as if she could physically dislodge Liam's paranoia. He was driving her crazy on every level. Liam's theories aside, it still didn't sit right with Isobel. "Are you sure it's wise? You don't know much about these people. Besides, I don't trust anything that's offered for free. They will make you pay somewhere down the line."

Melindi deflated. "But they said"—she hesitated—"anyway, I've always thought I was a good judge of character, and it feels right to me." She turned back to her washing.

Bel had hurt her friend. It would have been better to keep quiet. Now was probably also not the best time to bring up Melindi's choice of husband. At least she'd managed not to blurt that out too.

****

Bel took the wet plate from Liam and dried it. Mia was asleep upstairs but Bel wished the little girl was awake. She needed an excuse to get out of the kitchen and away from Liam's questions.

"All I'm asking, Bel, is why you haven't gone for counselling? After what you've been through, it would really help."

She saw her way out and took it.

"Speaking of counselling, you won't believe what Melindi has got herself into. You know that meeting she went to, when we babysat Ben and Lilly? The lady who runs the meeting has got her going every week now. On top of that, they've offered her free counselling. Seriously, who would fall for that?"

Bel put the plate on the pile in the cupboard and turned back to take another out of Liam's hand. She pulled, but he held on.

"Liam?"

He stood rooted, forehead creased, eyes locked on hers.

"It was a meeting for single moms, wasn't it?"

"Let go." Bel tugged and his fingers sprang open. His eyes darkened and she waggled a finger at him, "No, don't even go there. It is not that whole conspiracy thing. It's just a support group." She piled the plate and swung her cloth as a hint.

He hadn't moved a muscle since she'd mentioned the group.

Bel didn't want the conversation to come back to her. She kept talking. "My biggest fear for Melindi is that they'll rip her off. She thinks she's a good judge of character, but look at her choice of husband. Honestly, free counselling? Who does anything for free? There'll be a catch and I just hope Melindi sees it before it costs her."

Liam put a cup down and took her by the shoulders. "It could cost Melindi her life. This is exactly what I thought was happening. How can you not see it, Bel?"

Damp seeped through her sleeves from his soapy

hands. Isobel wanted to kick herself. She'd distracted him from analyzing her life, but had swatted another hive of bees in doing so.

"You know what? I'm going to prove to you that there is nothing sinister going on at that group. A bit of a scam, maybe even fraud, but murder and kidnapping? I don't think so. I'll prove it."

He lost a shade of colour. "Stay away, Bel. Please. I'll stop hounding you with this. I'll find somewhere safe for Mia. Anything you want. You don't have to get involved."

She wriggled free of his damp hands. "Too late."

****

Isobel's chair squeaked every time she moved. As if she didn't feel conspicuous enough already. She sighed and tried not to fidget. The single moms' group met in a tired church hall that had long since felt the loving caress of a paint brush. Heat and the humidity, so common to the south coast, had curled the ancient layers of paint into cracked bubbles a disturbing shade of fried egg white.

Melindi had dropped enough info in casual conversation for Isobel to pick up on and make contact with the group. They ran a number of meetings during the week. All Bel had to do was avoid the night Melindi went.

The moms chatted in little bunches, like burrs on a sock. Sitting amongst these ladies, Isobel was beginning to wish she'd listened to Liam. She might as well have *fraud* tattooed on her forehead.

Liam was convinced that coming to this group was as dangerous as slapping an elephant. If he could have successfully disguised himself as a woman, it would have been him sitting here now, rear end going numb from the effort of trying not to squeak.

The door leading deeper into the church opened. A slip of a woman with too little hair walked in. The limp bits that she did have hung off her scalp in frazzled dryness. She stopped off briefly at each group, trading a few quiet words before moving on. A stiff cotton dress in neutral colours fell like a shopping bag from her bony shoulders and swished around her legs as she walked. It was, without doubt, the wrong range of colours for her to be wearing.

It was a mismatch that made Bel itch between the shoulder blades. It didn't ring true. The woman peered over her thick glasses at the room full of ladies and clapped twice to get their attention.

"Come and sit, ladies. It is time to start."

The moms kept chatting as they found their seats, wallowing in the rare treat of adult conversation.

For most of them, Isobel would guess this was their only break from a week full of wiping runny noses, changing diapers, and feeding hungry mouths.

"Welcome to our first-timers. I hope you'll enjoy your time with us." She paused and smiled at them all in turn. It didn't seem to come from a warm place in her heart, but rather from the depths of some script that said it was a good time to smile. "My name is Loreen. We'd love to get to know you, so please tell us a bit about yourself and your children." With that, she turned her bug-under-a-microscope gaze onto Isobel and nodded for her to start.

Isobel's carefully rehearsed words turned purple with stage fright. Liam had insisted they go over her back-story until she could recite it backwards at two in the morning. That was all very well, but sitting here with all these eyes on her was another story altogether. The one thing they had managed to agree on, was to stay as close to the truth as possible.

The truth.

She could tell them the truth.

"Hi, my name is Isobel. The truth is I've only been a mom for the last few weeks. Though I guess I'm more like a substitute mommy."

Silence fell in the room as the words left her mouth. Yep, they were all paying attention now.

"I found a toddler abandoned on the beach. I'm looking after her till I can track down her real family. I'm here because I have no family of my own. I'm in way over my head and I need help."

A pale-skinned redhead was the first to break the silence that had fallen over the room. "That is so brave. We'd love to help wherever we can. Right, ladies?"

A chorus of warm encouragement swept over her as heads nodded and a few hands patted her knees.

One mom didn't agree. A delicate woman, all in shades of pink with 'Shawna' scrawled on her name tag, she spoke as if she'd swallowed half a bottle of vinegar. "You can't do this. That child must be handed over to the welfare to deal with. You can't play finders-keepers with a life."

Mere weeks back, Isobel would have been the first to agree. Now, the thought of Mia being taken from her was unbearable.

Shawna had touched a raw nerve.

"I know. You're right. I'm going to have to do the right thing. I just want to make sure she's recovered properly first."

The redhead *tsk*'d, annoyance colouring her voice.

"Shawna, stop being so proper. Isobel should get a medal for what she is doing. Seriously. How many people do you know who would take in a child like that?"

Throughout this exchange, Loreen sat silent, her face expressionless but for a faint flush that stained her cheeks. She waved the redhead back to her seat. "This is not an issue for us to sort out here. It will need to be put right, but this is not the place. We are here to encourage one another." *Encourage* came out of her mouth sounding like something one would classify right up there with salmonella poisoning. Something best avoided. Her slow drawl ground on and on.

Isobel shook her head to stay awake. She pinched her arm a couple of times, hoping to shake the lethargy that fogged her brain.

This woman was too much. She was saying all the right things, but there was no sign she believed what was coming out of her own mouth.

Isobel couldn't help yawning.

This lot was about as dangerous as a bowl of oatmeal. At room temperature. Served with a plastic spoon.

The door creaked open and clipped footsteps crossed the hall. A man in jeans and charcoal cotton shirt bent low, whispering in Loreen's ear. He glanced up and his gaze caught Isobel's. A strangle tingle tiptoed down her spine. Dark hazel eyes, faint silvery scar down one cheek. A vague smile played the corners of his mouth. She shut her eyes to breathe, and when she opened them he was leaving.

"Er, Isobel—did I get it right? We must talk. If you stay behind after the meeting, I may be able to help." Loreen regarded her, puzzlement creasing her brow.

Isobel sat upright as she heard her name. She blinked and pretended to rub an itchy eye to cover her sleepiness. "Pardon?"

"I want to help you. We'll talk after."

"OK, thank you."

The rest of the meeting was a blur of discussion and laughter which left Bel feeling nauseous. Liam had been so persistent last night, to the point of making her think maybe there was some fire to his smoke. But the longer she faced this washout Loreen and her group of average ladies, the more convinced Isobel was that they were barking up the wrong tree. In fact, right now, she was pretty sure that there was no tree at all.

Bel, stick it out. Surely after this, Liam would have to let it rest. This is the only way to prove him wrong in his suspicions.

Her interview with Loreen was as underwhelming as the rest of the meeting. Once they were alone, she gave Isobel a form to fill out and sat in brooding silence while Bel's pen squeaked its way through twenty random background questions. She felt oddly detached as she handed it over, as if she were rehearsing lines for a movie.

"We'll assess this and my people will get back to you in a few days."

Bel's unasked questions stayed that way as she was ushered out of the room and building with no chance given for anything more.

****

The call came through three days later.

Bel was trying to persuade Liam that it would be a good idea for him to go home. Just that morning, she stumbled out of bed in her half-awake state on the hunt for coffee. Forgetting that the door at the top of the stairs was locked, she'd smacked into it, head first. A purple bruise flowered instantly on her forehead.

The fact that he'd laughed made eviction by force a very attractive idea.

Every time she brought it up, he'd put her off saying it was as if they were living in two separate flats anyway, courtesy the locked door. This was always followed by mutterings that she never quite heard other than the word 'safe.'

Even now, as she answered the phone, he leaned against the wall with his arms across his chest and a cheeky eyebrow halfway to his hairline. It messed with her brain. It was time for him to go home.

"Isobel speaking."

"Loreen here, from the single moms' group."

Isobel felt a sudden need to make friends with the wall.

"I'm sorry, but we won't be able to take you into the counselling program. The criteria for acceptance is very specific, and I'm afraid you aren't quite right for it." She droned on for a while, but her words were buzzing noise in Bel's ears.

By the time they said good-bye, Bel had her hand on her hip, fingers drumming victory on her hip bone. She couldn't help grinning at Liam smugly. There was no way that the meeting she attended was a front for anything.

Liam was hovering over her like a nosy kid. "What's up?"

"Nothing. Absolutely *nothing*." It was all she could do to bite back the *I told you so!* that hovered on her tongue. "They don't think I qualify for counselling.

Doesn't that tell you something?"

"Not really. It just means they don't think that approach will work on you. They want Mia. There will be a backup plan. Make no mistake."

"Honestly, Liam? Why are you so obsessed?" Something deep and fragile within her snapped. "I've been through too much to live with your constant paranoia. I've got some serious thinking to do."

Mia started crying upstairs.

I can't do this.

Liam glanced upstairs and back, his eyes searching hers.

She looked away, shutting him out.

With a frustrated growl, he pushed past her and ran up the stairs two at a time. His leaving left nothing between her and the front door.

Fresh air.

She took the gap and bolted.

****

Upstairs in Bel's bedroom, Liam picked up Mia, set her on his lap, and dried her tears with his thumb. "There there, small stuff. All better."

She swatted his hands away, not ready to stop being grumpy just yet.

He held his hands in front of her, palms up. She fell for the bait and started slapping her palms on his, a two-year-old's version of a clapping game. The reprieve was brief. Four clumsy swats and she lost interest. "Where Mine?"

"She's coming now." Liam fought the smile off his lips. Laughing at that serious face would have been parental suicide. Mia never called Isobel "mom." She was "Mine," and that was the end of that. It made Liam melt. Every single time.

"Want Mine. Now." She slid off his lap and felt for his thumb, "Come wif. Find Mine."

She led him down the stairs, and he waddled after her like a duck on a string, hunched over to reach her hand. He nearly toppled down the stairs headfirst. How he managed to stay on his feet was nothing short of a miracle. This little girl was on a mission.

Mia stopped on the bottom step and called, "Mine?"

Liam saw the open door and knew they wouldn't find her.

Mia dragged him to the kitchen and the lounge.

Isobel's absence was too much for Mia. She flung herself onto the carpet and sobbed. Great gulping, heartbroken sobs, tiny fists thumping the innocent carpet.

Liam's heart could only take so much. "Come, Mia. I'm with you. Mine is coming now." He picked her up, dodging flying fists and feet. He held her close, forcing the flying bits to wave ineffectually behind him. The swing bench was the only solution he could think of for this inconsolable little mess. The cool air washed over them as he pulled open the door.

Stars littered the moonless sky, their fierce blaze reduced to a twinkle by the thousands of miles between space and their swing.

Mia stopped crying. She sat on his lap, blinking like an owl. "Schtars!" She pointed and patted his chest in excitement. "Schtar! Tinkle schtar!"

Liam was relieved to find the off button for her tears. He was only too happy to oblige if it meant that button stayed off. Clearing his throat, he got the swing going and launched into his own, rather mauled version of "Twinkle Twinkle Little Star" that somehow managed to involve pizza and a cow.

Mia didn't seem to mind. She relaxed in his arms, humming along here and there.

Even as nursery rhyme gibberish was coming out of his mouth, Liam's insides pressed upwards to the only One who could untie impossible knots. *Jesus, we need a breakthrough. For Mia. For Isobel. Keep her safe wherever she is. Show us what to do next.* He felt a warmth flood through him as he laid his gut bare. The hairs on his arms stood on end, and he knew that whatever came out of his mouth and heart now was being heard before the hosts of Heaven.

God Himself was listening.

At some point in the crossover from bovine pizza to powerful destiny, Mia nodded off. Safe and content.

17

Isobel ran. She left the house behind, not knowing where she was going. Ducking past a red pickup, her sneakered feet pounded the gravel. Her pace changed from I-gotta-get-out-of-here to the regular slap-slap of a normal jogger. *I'd give anything to be a normal jogger.* She ran through pools of light cast by overhead streetlights, through patches of inky blackness. Gravel became grass then became sand.

The crashing roar of the incoming tide broke around her as she dropped to her knees on the beach, breathing hard. Perspiration ran freely as she gasped for air. She slid to the side and then pulled up her knees, wrapping her arms around them.

The starlight did little to break the hold of darkness, but she welcomed the gloom. It enveloped her like a cloak, and it felt good. *What you can't see can't harm you.* Heightened by the blood rushing through her body, delivering fresh oxygen to depleted cells, her senses were in overdrive. She felt the prick of her unshaved legs.

Her priorities had shifted since Mia's arrival.

The sand beneath her rear was cold and damp, and sogginess seeped into the fabric of her denim shorts. The ocean hid in the dark, visible only as a deeper blackness than that which was all around her. The noise of the sea pounded in her ears, a seething mass of restless water—never ceasing, not moving forward, not receding. Endless tossing with little purpose.

Just like my life.

Isobel was alone for the first time in weeks, and her mind darted—a pond full of goldfish catching mosquitoes. She could feel herself breathing. Chest rising and falling. Predictable. Ordered. The goldfish slowly calmed, circling until they came to rest on one single conundrum. Mia.

It was too late to keep the walls up. Mia had shattered those completely and torn down the barricade to Bel's past in the same effortless flourish. Mia had ripped off the scab of the wound deep in Isobel that had never healed and somehow it didn't matter. It didn't matter because she loved the little blonde girl. It was a simple fact.

Keeping Mia...that was the challenge. If Liam was right, she was next in line to be kidnapped. So bizarre, so paranoid. Yet even if all that was just a delusion— child welfare would step in sooner or later. Either way, Isobel's heart was left quivering on the chopping block.

God, what am I going to do?

It felt as if her own thoughts answered her, but the tone was so different, the intent—the heart behind the words...

Fear not, My light has overcome the darkness...

The words trailed off as the moon broke through the bank of clouds camping on the horizon. Instantly, a thousand living sparkles set off a dazzling moonlit fire across the water. Waving shadows retreated to reveal a chorus line of palms swaying in the wind. By the silvery moonlight, she saw the curve of the beach off to the left, many footprints crisscrossing the sand at her feet.

Isobel staying on the beach, listening to the voice of the waves and wind as her mind tried to come up with a plan. Any plan.

My light has overcome the darkness...

At 3 AM she started shivering. The numbing cold of the sand joined forces with a sly wind that threaded goose bumps all down her spine. Her teeth started chattering, but she stayed put. She just wasn't ready to face what was waiting for her back home.

Fear not...

The words echoed in her head but her heart still fluttered.

If it was true, if Light truly had overcome the darkness—then she knew exactly what to do. But still she stayed there, frozen. Paralyzed by emotion and fear. Through the darkest hours of night, Isobel sat.

How do I know it was You speaking to me? It was probably my own messed up thoughts. I wish it was You, God. I wish there was Someone who knew what to do. Someone who could sort this mess out. Someone I could trust. God, are You real?

At that moment, the sun's rays blazed through the steely blue dawn sky, splitting it effortlessly into shards of darkness that diminished before her eyes.

From the moment the sun's light appeared, Isobel felt the warmth washing over her, into her. As the blazing ball inched higher in the sky, the heat of the rays intensified, seeping into her muscles. Raising her arms above her head, she clasped her hands and stretched, leaning left then right. She tucked her feet in underneath herself and rose. The sun had broken the freeze, and she found she could move once more. It was time to go home and set some things in motion.

****

Liam was fast asleep on the couch with Mia draped across his chest. His face was ragged, and he was snoring from the funny angle of his head.

Isobel felt a twinge of guilt for running and leaving him with Mia. She tiptoed through the lounge, praying for no creaks from the floor, to the bookshelf.

It took a bit of hunting. *Romeo and Juliet*. No. An entire shelf devoted to romance novels—definitely not. *National Geographic* magazines...

Aaah! There. She pulled a dog-eared leather-bound Bible from the shelf. She knelt on the floor, the book on her lap. Flipping to the concordance at the back, she opened up the index to *light*. Four columns of light verses. Finding the right one would take the rest of the year. Maybe *darkness* would be easier? Her heart sank as the musty pages fell open. Just as many. One caught her eye. She riffled back through the book. Reaching John chapter one, her finger traced down to verse five. *The light shines in the darkness, and the darkness has not overcome it.*

Wow.

A tingle shot down her spine.

There it was, black on white.

Tangible in her hands.

Not just a product of her fertile imagination.

She had to tell Liam. Setting the Bible down on top the bookshelf, she tiptoed over to him.

"Liam, wake up!" she hissed. Nothing. Prodding his arm did nothing. She patted his cheek, and he turned his head towards her hand, breathed deeply, and smiled.

You've got to be kidding me!

"Liam!"

His eyes shot open, and he would have sat up and sent Mia flying but for Isobel's arm across his shoulders. It took all her force to peg him.

"Oh, my neck." He groaned and tried to move his head. He sat up gingerly, one arm holding Mia tight, the other attempting to rub life back into his stiff spine. He eyed her through one open eye. The man was a mess. "You're back."

"I shouldn't have taken off."

Mia squirmed in his arms, shifting herself sideways to a more comfortable position. She drew in a deep breath and settled.

"No matter. There's a lot going on. You want to talk?"

"I think God spoke to me."

She caught him mid-yawn.

"Actually I know He did." She couldn't stop a grin from tugging at the corners of her mouth.

"What?" He was wide-awake now. He pulled himself upright, causing Mia to slide down his chest. She woke with a start and was winding up for a good sob when she saw Bel. She clambered off Liam, nearly falling in her sleep-befuddled state.

"Mine! Mine back!" She launched herself at Bel in delight, pushing her off balance. They landed with a thud that nearly knocked the wind out of Isobel. Mia's short arms just made it around Bel's neck and she rained kisses on her face. Isobel was helpless beneath this onslaught. Laughter bubbled through her.

Liam rolled his shoulders and winced as he tried moving his head from side to side. He looked a right wreck.

Seeing him all mussed up and out of sorts turned

Bel to jelly. She couldn't keep the grin off her face, "I should have warned you; these couches are not great for sleeping on."

"You are actually enjoying this! Good grief, woman. I'll have to sort you out."

Bel didn't answer. Mia was all over her, chattering away like a squirrel on fermented nuts. "Mia, go fetch your soft monkey. He's upstairs."

"Onkey?"

"Yes! Go fetch him."

"OK."

She toddled off, happy to be on a mission.

My heart on a chopping block, waiting for the knife to fall...

"So what is this about God?"

Isobel brushed the tears off her face and wiped them on her shorts. Beach sand showered off in all directions. More to clean.

"I think I had a conversation with Him. On the beach. It was strange, but not weird-strange. More amazing-strange. If you know what I mean?" Her nose wrinkled as she tried to string the words together in an order that made some sort of sense.

"So what did He say?"

"Firstly, you have to move back home!"

18

Liam faced his consulting room door with all the reluctance of a turkey before Thanksgiving. He was not a happy man. Isobel had been stubborn from the start. Trying to convince her to be careful now that she'd heard from God was nothing short of impossible. Against his every instinct, he was back home. Bel was convinced it was all over, determined to carry on with normal life. The knot in his stomach was one worthy of a boy scout's badge. How could this possibly end well?

Bel saw no reason to hide any longer. She'd even mentioned adoption.

His key stuck in the lock. He pushed it down as he turned and the lock popped open. Things are easier once one has the knack. He pocketed the key. If only he could get through to Isobel. His gut said the criminal element was still out there.

Mia had slipped through the kidnapper's clutches once, and he was sure to want her back.

So here he was, powerless to help. Unable to protect Isobel or Mia. A knight stripped of his horse, lance, and shield. With a sigh, he pushed open the door to his rooms.

****

Mia's juice bottle slipped out of the bag and rolled towards the street. Bel hooked it with her foot and bit back a purple word. She put the bottle back in its pocket and yanked on the zipper to keep it there. Whichever way she pulled the zip, the gaping hole remained gaping. Broken. Just perfect.

It was nearly midday and they hadn't managed to leave the house yet. Mia had to be changed twice during the morning, once for a porridge slop the size of a small country and the second time for more than half her cup of chocolate milk down her front. She seemed thoroughly intent on wearing her food, a trend that did not sit well with Isobel.

After mopping up oats and milk, Bel had to find a new set of clothes herself. Applying sunblock was a nasty affair that ate up another half an hour. Getting a hat tied onto Mia to protect her fair scalp gobbled some more time. Now, two hours after she'd first tried to walk out the front door, they were both as ready as they'd ever be. And the zip was broken on her bag. There was no way she was going back inside to change bags.

Standing in the blazing sunlight, Isobel didn't recognise herself. She had spent the last ten years avoiding children of every shape and size. Now here she was, an internet list of the best kid-friendly places to visit in Scottburgh clutched firmly in one hand and the chubby hand of a two-year-old in the other. Bel had asked Melindi to come with them, but she had other plans.

A leisurely stroll to the park, some playing...a cautious shiver of delight crept over Bel. Such a simple thing, yet it had been denied her for so long she'd convinced herself she didn't want it.

They walked at the pace of Mia's short legs, chatting about the flowers and sidewalk ants and all the woof-woofs they passed.

Mia's hand was damp with perspiration and she gripped so tight it pinched, but Isobel relished the feeling.

Halfway to the park, Mia tugged on Bel's shorts' leg. "Uppy." It was not a question, but a command.

"No, Mia. I can't carry you. Come on. It's not that far."

Mia whimpered and gave a pre-tantrum foot stamp. "Uppy!" Her arms stuck in the air, homing missiles aimed at Bel.

She knew Mia well enough to know the signs. Isobel picked her up, cradled her to her chest, trying to distribute the weight as much as possible, and clasped her hands together beneath Mia's bottom.

By the time they got to the park, Isobel was sure she was red in the face, definitely drenched in sweat, and her arms ached as if she'd caber-tossed a baby elephant.

The park stretched the length of an entire block, filled with enough equipment to keep a small zoo full of monkeys happy. Climbing, swinging, hanging, or falling — this park catered to it all.

The moment they arrived, Mia's energy returned miraculously. She wriggled out of Bel's arms and scampered towards the highest slide in the park. Bel caught her just as she was starting to climb.

"Uh-uh! Let's find something more your size."

It took some fierce persuading to get Mia to lose interest in the giant slide. A sickly green see-saw balanced on an oversized cement mushroom caught her attention. It was built for tiny bottoms, with extra safety bars to hold in arms that weren't quite strong enough.

Bel would never fit in the other side, but one foot did the trick and she pumped her leg up and down while Mia shrieked in delight.

It soon lost its charm, and Mia found a sand pit. Relieved to be off see-saw duty, Isobel settled under a nearby tree, enjoying the cool shade. She closed her eyes, revelling in the peace. When she opened them, Mia was gone.

A few heart-stopping seconds later, she saw her at the bottom of the ladder to the tall slide.

"No! Mia!" Bel ran. She was too slow and got to the slide as Mia reached the top. Mia must have realized how high she was. She froze and started sobbing.

Bel didn't think twice. She climbed the ladder, heart in her throat. Her arms were shaking by the time she got to Mia, and she slipped an arm around her chest as the little girl's grip failed.

The jolt gave Mia a fright and she started screaming.

"I got you."

There was no going down the stairs with only one arm to climb with. The only way to go was down the slide. Bel managed to manoeuvre herself and Mia off the steps and onto the slide. It was a simple matter of sliding down now. There was only one problem. Her bum didn't fit. Bel wiggled to free herself and Mia slipped out of her grip. She slid all the way down as Bel watched in horror, picking up speed as she went. At this rate, she would shoot off the end and break something.

"Mia! No!"

As the scream left Isobel's throat, a man ran up and caught Mia midair.

Bel stretched out on the slide, turning onto her side. She slipped free and made it to the bottom within seconds of Mia's rescue.

"I believe this belongs to you?"

She turned to her rescuer and her breath caught in her throat. Eyes of deep hazel caught and held hers. His wispy blonde fringe jutted out from a crew cut that played off a tan that was just the right shade of outdoors. A faint scar ran the length of one cheek, barely visible. He wore his war wounds well. All vaguely familiar. *From where?*

"Thank you." She took Mia who stopped crying and buried her face in Bel's neck.

"No problem. She moves fast."

"I know! I just closed my eyes for a moment and she bolted. Thank you again. If she'd slipped…"

"Happy to help. Sometimes I'm in the right place at the right time." He bent down and picked up her purse. "This yours too?"

"Oh, my word, yes!" She felt red infuse her cheeks. "The zip on my bag is broken, I never even realized it had fallen out. Thank you." She took it and pushed it deep in, towards the bottom of her bag in the hopes that it would stay there. Her fingers sank into something squishy. *What?*

Mia had deposited her half-eaten chocolate marshmallow egg into Bel's bag. It was now impaled on Bel's fingers, webbing sticky underneath her finger nails. Charming.

"Don't mention it." A belly laugh danced in his eyes. He kept it in, winked at her, and walked off chuckling.

Licking her fingers, she watched him leave, feeling as if she knew him. No, that wasn't quite it. More like her knew her. That single thought unsettled her completely.

****

Liam pulled on a pair of sneakers that he should have retired years ago. His toe poked through a hole in the front and the tread was worn clean through in places.

This is how I feel. Worn out. Worn through.

He tugged on a black sweater, black as his mood. The last two weeks had been nothing short of murder. Bel had distanced herself from him completely. She wouldn't take his calls. He was pretty sure that if they were heading towards each other on the street, she would cross over to avoid him. He could understand, in his head, where she was at. It just didn't help his heart much.

He cracked eggs into a pan next to three slim rashers of bacon. It also didn't help that he'd seen her being dropped off at The Studio by some blonde guy. He kept telling himself that he wasn't jealous. He had no claim on her or Mia. All he knew was that his gut reacted badly to seeing her with that man.

Liam was a man of action, used to being in control. His job required that much of him all the time. His quick action had saved more lives than he cared to keep track of. He turned a sliver of bacon. It sizzled in the pan, and he stepped back to avoid the spatter of hot oil. But now? He could do nothing. Just watch the same real life horror movie play out all over again. It was killing him.

The phone rang. Detective Nass.

"Brigs, how's our girl? Still safe?"

"Only just. Please tell me you're ready to step in."

"No, but we are getting closer. The kids that vanished never made it to the welfare office. Whoever is masterminding this manages to hijack them before any official involvement from the police or Social Services."

"That's not good news." Instead of hunting through a goldfish bowl, they now had to search the sea.

"It's progress. Keep them both alive and in Scottburgh. I'm working as fast as I can."

The line went dead. Liam sighed. And he had no idea where the idea came from. One moment he was perplexed—in despair—and the next moment a light had gone on and the seed of a plan began turning in his brain.

Liam turned the heat off on the stove and set the half-cooked food aside. He needed to think this through before morning. If he timed it just right, his plan might work.

****

Bel was humming as she sprinkled sesame seeds over the teriyaki chicken that had just come out of the oven. How long had it been since she felt so light inside?

Mia was in the highchair, feeding herself fish fingers and mash. She'd eaten all her peas first, one at a time, popping them in her mouth with chubby fingers. She'd starting on the mash with a spoon, but decided that her hands worked better, wiping them on her shirt in between every mouthful.

Bel sighed. She had twenty minutes to get herself

dressed, and now half of those would be taken up bathing Mia.

"Come on, fairy. Let's get you clean."

Mia protested loudly as Bel picked her up out of the high chair. She wasn't yet finished playing with her mash.

"Not today, Mia. Please."

Mia started crying and wriggling to get out of Bel's grip. Bel held on and carried her octopus baby upstairs, arms and legs flailing wildly.

By the time she was clean and dressed, Bel had enough time to throw on a summery shift boasting fuchsias in shades of magenta and turquoise. She ran a brush through her hair and some lip gloss over her lips as the doorbell rang. Her feet slid into coppery slip-ons and then she hurried downstairs, leaving Mia engrossed in an unintelligible conversation between her two sheep slippers.

Isobel swung the door back, suddenly breathless, not sure if it was from the dash downstairs or the man leaning on the porch pillar cradling chrysanthemums and a bottle of red. Bel didn't drink wine, but she glossed over that small fact, basking in the light of his approving smile.

"These are for you."

She stood back to usher him in, taking the flowers. Maybe chrysanthemums weren't just for funerals, after all. She pulled off the extra leaves and then popped the flowers in a vase. She spread them out. Even that pushed her flower arranging skills to the limit.

By the time she carried her arrangement through to the lounge, Roric had switched off the main light and set the lamp to its dimmest.

Isobel swallowed hard, deposited the flowers on

the bookshelf, and retreated to the bright kitchen.

Mia was singing loudly upstairs. "Baa-baa back ship, 'ave oo anyoool…"

Roric came through to the kitchen with the bottle. "Corkscrew?"

Isobel had one from her twenty-first. It had been used for non-alcoholic champagne on that evening and had done a fantastic job of gathering dust since. Since the night she'd been drugged, she couldn't face anything that removed her from her senses. She dug the corkscrew from the back of the drawer and handed it over.

Wine glasses—now there was a problem.

"These will have to do." Tall glasses, intended for anything but wine. Isobel felt like a teenager playing at being a big girl.

Roric took them with no comment and was pouring when Mia made her grand entrance.

"Mine, looks!" She rounded the corner with a flourish.

Isobel had left her makeup drawer open, and Mia had helped herself. Thick black eyeliner criss-crossed her face, her nose a solid beak of black. Crimson lipstick covered her forehead in a patch that could pass for a fatal wound. Deep purple eye-shadow circles on each cheek completed the ghoul look. Isobel hung suspended between absolute horror and utter amusement. After a look at Roric's face, horrified won.

Mia frowned at Roric as if he'd just shot one of her stuffed toys.

It took a full forty-five minutes and a bath ring to get her clean and tucked into bed. By the time Bel came down, the chicken was sulking and half the bottle of wine was in Roric.

"I don't even know where to start," Isobel said. "I'm so sorry."

"That's the thing about kids. Your life is no longer your own."

"Can't argue with that." *But it was so worth it. Right?* She sank onto the couch looking forward to some mellow conversation involving more than single syllable words.

Swallowing the last mouthful from his glass, Roric put it down and got up to leave. "I need to go."

Isobel didn't have the heart to argue.

Roric leaned in close, lifted her chin with his fingers and kissed her full on the lips, lingering for a breath too long.

She wasn't expecting it and it threw her.

He pulled away just as quickly, turning to the door. He stopped at the open Bible on the bookshelf. It was still open on the light and darkness verse she'd found. She'd left it there on purpose, rereading it every time she walked by.

"You've been reading fairy stories, I see."

Still reeling from being kissed, she struggled to get a word out. A full coherent sentence was not even an option.

He slammed the cover closed. "Though I must admit there is a whole lot of truth hidden in these pages. Not the kind you'd expect to find though." He laughed then, mocking—at once a comedian and an adoring audience rolled into one body.

Bel fell silent; his jokes washed shame over her.

His laughter cut short and the slightest headshake convinced her that she was beyond hope. Roric let himself out, leaving her floundering in the middle of the lounge wondering why life was so cruel.

19

Bel was early to drop Mia at Melindi's. Her friend was distracted. More than that, unhappy.

Bel stepped carefully to avoid bits of Lego. The normal happy clutter had doubled, bordering on flat-out chaos.

Safely in the kitchen, Melindi spooned instant coffee into cups of steaming water, added sugar, milk, and forgot to stir.

Bel pulled the cup towards her and fetched her own spoon from the drawer.

Melindi wrinkled her nose apologetically. "Sorry. My mind is elsewhere."

Bel waved off her apology. "Are you sure you're ready for this little handful today?"

Melindi shrugged, but the frown remained settled between her brows. When she did speak, she sounded off. "Are you sure you want to leave Mia with me?"

"Melindi, what's up? Are you feeling sick?

"It's nothing, really. It seems that all the decisions I've made lately are the wrong ones." She sipped coffee and put it down in disgust. "Give me that spoon." She reached over and took it.

"Something has happened. You can tell me."

"No, not at all. I'm just..." She trailed off, not finding the words to convey what was going on inside. She checked her watch. "You'd better get a move on. You are going to be late."

****

Liam hung around the stairwell feeling like a stalker. He'd watched from a distance as Isobel arrived. When she didn't come down again he moved into position. Without thinking, he hitched his collar up, peering over the top of it, trying to blend in.

A car door slammed in the parking lot and his nerve gave in. He turned tail to leave, but then turned back. Something had to change or he'd go loopy. He was trying to decide if he should leave, when three ladies came around the corner, nearly bumping into him.

"Morning!" As wide as she was high, the short lady grinned sunshine at him from her round face, while her friend in grey frowned and hurried past, clutching her bag closer to her chest.

Another lady with a mop of hair that stuck out like feathers on a duster was digging in her bag. She muttered something about *again* and walked straight into him, grinding his toes into the pavement. "Oh my! I'm sorry! Did I hurt you?"

Liam gave his toes an experimental squeeze and winced. "I'll live." He plunged in before he could change his mind. "Are you ladies in Isobel's class?"

The foot squasher was still fretting over his foot and her open handbag, but the round lady answered for them all. "We are. What's it to you?" She looked him up and down critically, as if trying to figure out which box he fitted into in her head.

Liam turned down the collar on his jacket and ran nervous fingers through his hair. "Isobel is in danger, and I need your help."

The lady in grey stepped back out of the doorway. "What's going on?"

"Ladies, there is a coffee shop across the road from here. Meet me after your lesson." He eyed one skeptical face after another and added, "Please?"

The ladies left with no promises and he sat down on the bottom step as if all the strength had drained from his legs. Lost in thought, he didn't hear the footsteps until they came to rest in front of him. He recognized the sneakers.

"What are you doing here?" Isobel asked.

"I just wanted to see how you are."

"I'm great. Never been happier. I need to get back to my class."

"Mia? How is she?"

"Mia is fine. Liam, please."

"And the guy? Who is he? You need to be careful—"

"Stop! I don't want to hear it. I am over your paranoia. I can't live there. I won't." She turned on her heel and ran back upstairs, leaving behind whatever it was she had come down to fetch.

Liam ignored the writhing mass of toxic doubt that churned behind his ribs. Maybe it was all in his head, blown out of proportion because it had hit too close to home. *God, maybe I should give up. I am doing no good. Just causing more heartache. My own heart is raw and bleeding. Who can see straight with a heart in that state?*

He heard the words, not with his ears, but reverberating in every fibre of his being. A fierce response of a love stronger than death...

You cannot give up. I never give up on you.

****

It was the darkest corner of the coffee shop. The shop itself favoured feminine clientele. A lady's touch dripped from every blossomed curtain and each delicate tie-back. Soft violins filled the air with melancholy.

Determined to keep his voice low, he'd squeezed in enough chairs around one tiny table for them all to sit close. He could only hope the finely carved chair under his rear would hold him up long enough to recruit some back up. All six of them were crammed in, elbow to elbow, hunched forward like conspirators on a mission.

Introductions were over and Kez-Lyn was the first to speak. "Should I come sit on your lap, Mischa? It would be more comfortable than this."

Round Mischa was more red-in-the-face than usual. "Honestly, Kez? No. Just no."

"Sorry, ladies." Liam wore the sheepish look that had rescued him from the brunt of many a teacher's irritation back in the day.

Savannah, being more comfortable in sweat than the others, was quick to pull their focus back. "We're here because we love Bel. What's up?"

Liam squirmed, knowing how crazy this would sound. "I have no proof, but there is something going on in this town that has put Isobel and Mia in the path of terrible danger. She thinks I'm paranoid and won't listen. I was hoping you could make her see sense."

"You'll need to tell us more than that, sunshine." Jules spread her perfectly manicured hands, fingers beating rhythmic impatience on the table.

Liam nodded. "Babies have been taken. The pattern is always the same—single mom, mom disappears, and the baby is supposedly taken into the welfare system. I think Mia was next in line to go, but Bel happened to be there to intercept the pickup and mess up the plan. Now, I think they are after her. Bel doesn't see it; she doesn't want to hear. I can understand completely—after all she's been through. But I can't do nothing and see this happen all over again."

Jules frowned. "What do you mean, *again*?"

Maggie had sat quietly through the whole exchange, watching. She sat forward in her chair, regarding Liam with the intensity of a mom smelling smoke on her teenager. "Why does this matter so much to you? You care for her, don't you?"

Jules wasn't satisfied. "No, wait. Maggie, just give me a moment. You said *again*. I heard you. What do you mean?"

"I'm a doctor. It's my job to care for the people in this town. That's all." A muscle twitched in Liam's jaw.

Kez-lyn was shaking her head. "I don't know ladies. If he can't be honest with us, why should we trust him?"

Mischa moved her chair back an inch. "I agree." She glanced at her watch. "I need to get home."

Chairs scraped on the floor, singing a sour chorus of doom.

Something snapped deep inside Liam. A tightly coiled grip on the past, on his emotions. He erupted. "What do you ladies want to hear me say? That I love Isobel?"

Silence. No chairs. No movement.

"I do." A mere whisper, yet a shockwave of truth rippled through him.

Maggie sat down. "So what can we do?"

****

Mia had a plastic silver crown in a death grip. She would not budge.

Isobel pulled her out the way and squashed herself against the neat rows of tinned baked beans to let a lady and her trolley rattle past. The shop was claustrophobically full.

Mia held up the crown with eyes that sparkled.

Isobel had no intention of buying the gaudy silver mess. She had spoken nicely, tried a bribe, now she was on the verge of outright begging. The crown was cheap enough: she could easily have bought it for Mia without affecting the budget. The issue here was control.

Roric had warned her that this would be coming. *Stick to your guns. Don't give in. Show her who is boss.*

"Mia, put that down. We're going."

"Want it. Peez, Mine?"

"No. Not today. Come now."

"Peez, Mine?"

To hear such a tiny person do her best at asking nicely was enough to melt Bel.

But Roric's warnings rang loud in her head. *Establish your authority now, or you will have lost the battle. You'll be twisted around her little finger forevermore.*

Torn between her instincts and his advice, Bel lost it.

"No! Stop it now!"

Mia's eyes shot wide, filled with tears, and she threw the crown with such force, that it bounced.

Bel grabbed her by the arm, left her full shopping trolley there in the aisle, and pulled her towards the exit.

Mia lost her footing and fell on her knees, grazing them. Blood ran down her leg, staining her socks.

Bel could feel the eyes of the shoppers on her. She wanted to run. Leave Mia and run.

A purple-rinsed granny shuffled past in tweed and old lady shoes, offering a lavender scented tissue.

Embarrassed beyond herself, Bel waved the tissue away, picked up Mia—which made her scream—and aimed herself at the nearest exit. By the time she got to the car, she was shaking with emotion.

Mia was red in the face and still screaming.

One thought stared Bel down like a bull to her red flag. As much as she'd longed for motherhood, it was time to get honest. *I am not cut out for this.*

20

Bel was on her second round of crumb wiping for the morning. A tiny crumb had missed her first sweep through the kitchen, and that was enough to necessitate a second wipe down.

A drizzly grey day lurked outside the kitchen window, seeping gloom through the open curtains.

Bel sighed. She missed the sun. She missed the sun outside her window and inside her head. Her heart.

She told herself that life was good. Roric was systematically helping her to work through the emotional baggage and wrap it up in neat boxes. Far better than the chaos that she was used to when her feelings were left to run amok. Yet somehow, there was a strange disconnect happening that she couldn't put her finger on. She had tried, but the closest she could come to explaining it was that she was happy in her head, but her heart had been left behind.

Rochelle's classes still took up her mornings, but it was all about the techniques now, no heart connection. She couldn't afford to let the ladies come close. Not until she'd sorted out what was going on properly anyway. The evening classes were a thing of the past.

Rochelle had tried to talk her into coming back, but Isobel had dodged the offer—using Harry as her justification for staying away.

Life really was better like this. She had much more control.

Mia was squealing at a seal with his whiskered face and soulful eyes when Bel became aware of being watched for the first time.

The aquarium was crowded, even for a Saturday morning.

Roric was with them and had a protective arm around Mia's shoulder. She had never really taken to him, but the excitement of meeting a seal for the first time had overpowered her usual tortoise-like withdrawal.

Bel turned toward a flash of movement out the corner of her eye. Whoever it was had moved in behind a ghost crab information board. All she could see were jean-clad legs ending in ostrich-leather boots next to a floral skirt and shoes straight from the sixties.

I'm getting as paranoid as Liam was.

They moved on to the jellyfish display. A thick, metre-wide column of glass stretched up toward the high ceiling. The jellyfish floated inside the see-through pillar, exquisite beadwork of living flesh, trailing long tentacles that drifted with the current. Glowing alien-like under the fluorescent lighting—the tiny creatures where breathtaking in their beauty.

Bel shuddered as she thought of one of those tentacles wrapping around her. So beautiful, but so painful. Through the display, Bel caught sight of movement on the other side of the room. It was jeans and flowers again, backs toward her, staring deeply into the seahorse tank. Why they should stand out in a room bustling with bodies, Bel had no idea. Then she saw it. The furtive glance they sent her way, turning back quickly when they saw her looking.

She squinted through the gloom, trying to see

more.

Mia ran around a corner to the manta ray display. Bel followed, casting a last glance at her spies before moving out of view. There was something familiar about the two of them.

Roric took her hand. "Everything all right? You aren't with us."

"Watch Mia for me, will you? I think I see someone I know."

"Sure." Mia had found the clownfish further along, and he joined her while Bel stayed at the corner—jellyfish in sight.

Sure enough, her two tails were peering around the display, looking worried. Not giving the jellyfish a second look, they hurried over to where Bel was hiding.

She stepped out as they came around the corner. "What are you ladies doing here?"

Savannah and Kez-Lyn jumped in shock.

Kez recovered first. "It's a lovely day for the aquarium, don't you think?"

Savannah was nodding, wide-eyed in agreement.

"Without your kids? Ladies? What is going on?"

Kez-Lyn was peering around. "Where is Mia?"

"Mia is fine. Roric is watching her so that I could find out what on earth you two are up to. If I didn't know better, I would say you were stalking me." She stuck her hand on her hip and looked from one to the other.

Neither of them paid any attention.

"Come on. Let's go find her." Savannah sounded quietly panicked.

Kez-Lyn nodded. "Yes! Good idea. I've missed her. Come on, Bel."

The two ducked past Isobel and headed toward the clownfish.

She had to run to catch up.

They found Mia with her face pressed up against a tank of prickly sea urchins.

"Mine! Look!" Her chubby finger poked the glass, leaving tiny fingerprints. "Owey!"

"Those would be sore, Mia. You are quite right. Roric, these ladies are from my art class." She introduced them and cringed as Kez, dressed in her hippiest florals, eyed him up and down.

Savannah was a shade more civil in her greeting, before turning all her attention to Mia. "Look at those spiky urchins, Mia. That one is purple."

"Poople?" Mia tapped the glass and pressed her nose up so hard her teeth clinked on the cold surface.

Roric moved her away with a frown. "Careful now." He was smiling again, though, as he turned back to greet the ladies. Seemingly oblivious to the undercurrents, he greeted them by name as if etching their names into his memory.

What was going on with these ladies?

Over the next two weeks, her art class ladies gate-crashed her dates with Roric with tedious regularity. There was dinner at the Italian restaurant on First Street, an afternoon visit to the zoo, tea at the Wild Bird Park. Whenever she confronted them, they brushed her off, saying what a small world it was, especially in Scottburgh.

Liam had backed off, much to her relief. The last time she had seen him was their argument outside the art studio. She told herself that it was better this way, but her heart sank when Mia went looking for him.

She wandered through the house calling for her

Liam. At those times, her decision haunted her.

****

Liam wiped the perspiration off his forehead with the back of his hand. He adjusted his headphones and whispered into the microphone, "All set, ladies? Testing."

Crackling, silence, then Jules answered, "Coming through loud and clear. We are in place, good to go."

They'd chosen her to wear the mic as it fit snugly behind the lapel of her denim jacket. She was also the most likely to remain calm under pressure.

Liam peeped out the window of the makeshift surveillance vehicle that he'd thrown together. He'd borrowed a minivan with tinted windows from a musician patient of his and kitted it out with a radio transmitter and receiver. He'd parked across the street from Bel's house and used the spare key to let the craft clubbers in. It was time for some serious intervention, but he knew that his presence would send Bel off in the opposite direction. So he'd briefed the ladies and bowed out gracefully.

As for the ladies, the changes in Bel had them sick with worry, and they seemed more than ready to step in.

He heard a car.

Bel was pulling into the driveway.

"She's home. Ladies, do your best. Her safety and Mia's life are at stake."

"We'll do whatever we can, Doctor." Jules sounded calm. Too calm.

There was nothing more he could do. Just trust them to persuade Bel. And pray.

The radio went silent. His heart was beating so loudly, he could hear the thump-thump echoing in his head. He sneaked a glance out the window.

Bel was unlocking the front door. She let Mia in first, then followed and closed the door behind them.

He waited.

"Good heavens! What are you ladies doing here?" Static crackle distorted the signal, but he could still make out the words.

Jules spoke. He could hear every word as if she were standing in front of him. "Isobel, this is an intervention."

"Intervention? Intervention for what? Are you all crazy?"

"We want you to be careful of Roric. We don't trust him."

Liam groaned. Subtlety was not Jules's strongpoint.

"Have you been talking to Liam? I would expect this kind of thing from him. Not from you ladies. What has he been telling you? Is he the reason you've been tailing me?"

He had to grin at that. Isobel knew him far better than she thought she did.

"Bel, listen. You have a way of creeping into a person's heart."

Liam strained to hear, but he couldn't make out who was speaking.

"And that's what you've done with us. We love you, otherwise we wouldn't be here."

They all started talking at once, muffling the signal.

Liam ground his teeth. *One at a time, ladies!*

Isobel spoke above the noise. "Here's the thing

that I don't get. I feel more together now than I have in years. I can't see why you lot would think that is so bad."

Was she angry? Upset? He couldn't tell. More than anything, he wished he could be there to look in her eyes and make sure she was OK.

"Together is not always good."

Softly spoken, maybe Maggie?

"To us, it feels like you are slowly freezing over. The joy and light that were such a part of you is fading. Your life wasn't perfect, Bel. You were dealing with challenges, pain...but in it all, you were gloriously alive. Real. Present. We're losing you."

Silence.

Liam felt a bead of sweat run down the nape of his neck. This van was suffocating. Still nothing. He was about to start fiddling with knobs and cables when Isobel spoke.

There was no mistaking the quiet fury in her voice. "It's easy for all of you to look fondly on the mess that I was. You didn't have to live it. So maybe I've buried my emotions. You know what? Because of it, I might just survive. You all have no right to come in here under the banner of 'love' and try and take me back to the disaster that I was before. I will not go."

"We never meant to hurt you, Bel."

Liam couldn't tell who was speaking, but he could hear thick pain in the voice.

Jules spoke. "Isobel, we'll leave now. But before we go, promise us you will watch out for two things, and when they start to happen—which they will—come and find us. Please?" Jules was calm and detached.

Good girl.

"What things?"

Knowing Bel, she'd pay attention with the hopes of proving them all wrong.

Liam didn't care, as long as she took them in.

"The first is a subtle undermining of your skills as a mom. A dropped hint here and there. Nothing obvious. Just enough to make you doubt your instincts. At some point he'll suggest a night out without Mia."

"But we've done that. Melindi babysits. I don't see the problem."

Jules floundered.

Liam grabbed the mic and whispered even though he could have shouted and Bel wouldn't have heard the feed into Jules's ear.

"Tell her it will be on a night Melindi can't babysit. He will offer to find a babysitter."

Jules was coughing to buy time. She ended her cough with a whispered *got it*. "Melindi won't always be there. He'll offer to find a babysitter."

Silence.

"You are all wrong, you know." Her words trailed off at the end. A glimpse through the tinted glass showed the front door swinging open. They were coming out.

"We love you, Bel."

The only response was the front door swinging shut behind them as they walked down the path. They had done everything they could.

All that remained was to pray. Pray and trust.

****

They were a few minutes early for their lesson.

Liam found the others ladies downstairs and they

squashed into the lift together. "Ladies, you have to stop tailing Isobel."

"Why?" Kez wrinkled her nose.

Maggie frowned. "I thought that was one of our better ideas. I'm surprised you didn't ask us to in the first place."

"I liked it, too." Savannah shrugged. "She is still mad at us, I'm sure."

Liam was torn. "As much as I love knowing that you have your eyes on her every move, when it comes to that man, we can't risk him getting suspicious or put your lives at risk. Or your families. Think about it. You ladies aren't quite stealth material yet. You're just not subtle enough."

The lift shuddered to a stop and the ladies walked into the studio to find Rochelle, no Isobel.

Rochelle's voice filtered through to the lift as Liam punched the button to go down. "Morning, ladies. I'm sorry to have to tell you that Isobel is no longer with us. I'll be taking your classes from now on until I find a suitable replacement." She carried on talking, allowing no time for questions, taking them step-by-step through the process of fabric painting a cushion.

****

Mia was crying in a high chair. Her eyes were red-rimmed and damp with tears. A red hand mark was beginning to show on her thigh were Roric had smacked her for not wanting to finish her hot dog.

Bel had never agreed with the concept of forcing a child to eat beyond the point where they no longer felt hungry. But then, maybe Roric was right. She needed to learn the value of food and not to waste it. Isobel shut off the voice in her head that disagreed. He was right of course. He always was.

She checked her watch. Her ladies would be washing brushes and tidying up by now. Part of her wanted to be there, elbow to elbow rinsing off paint and laughing at the comments flying. She brushed away the thought. Now was not the time to get soft, not with the progress she was making.

"Isobel!" Roric was glaring at her.

"What?"

"Did you hear a word I was saying?"

"I'm so sorry. I was just—"

"You need to think about what kind of example you're setting. You can't expect Mia to focus when you are forever drifting off somewhere in your head."

Isobel felt the familiar wave of embarrassment wash through her. She really wasn't cut out to be a mom. *You really aren't... what?* I'm not any good at being a mom. *Says who?* She thought for a moment. Roric. He knows about these things. *Oh, really?*

The thought hovered in her mind as she turned toward him. He had finished correcting her and the charm was back. It was this side of him that she found irresistible—confident, self assured. Yet that one simple question hung in the air between them like a fog—a truth serum for her mind.

It was almost funny.

She needed time to think.

"I think I'm coming down with something. Can we postpone?" She put her hands on her belly and wasn't lying. "My stomach is in knots."

He brushed back her hair and ran a hand along her jaw line, his touch cool. "Of course. Look after yourself, my dove. Get to bed early. I've managed to book tickets for The Playhouse tomorrow night. You know the show you were raving about? Collaboration of live art on stage: dance and music? You can't be sick."

"I told you I can't make tomorrow night. I don't have anyone to look after Mia."

"It's part of my treat. I've organised someone."

Isobel picked Mia up out of the high chair and held her close. Mia reached down and pulled at the top button of Bel's blouse. Isobel absently covered the button with her own hand to prevent Mia's clever fingers from wielding the new skill they had mastered.

The light was off in the kitchen and she kept it that way as she watched Roric walk down the garden path and let himself out the gate.

Mia was quiet in her arms. Thinking back over the last few weeks, Bel realized she hadn't said much at all, reverting back to staring at the world silently through sombre eyes.

Isobel felt hot tears prick as she snuggled Mia against her, as if her body warmth could erase the darkness she'd been succumbing to. One question from God—there was no denying it was Him—and light had flooded into her, exposing the twisted truth. That was too close. Her arms around Mia were shaking.

"I'm so sorry, my little Mia. So sorry." She kissed the top of Mia's hair, breathing in her scent, her softness.

Mia's arms stayed hanging at her sides.

Isolation swamped Isobel. She had alienated all her friends, taken a torch to the connections as if they were origami bridges. No, not all. There was still one.

She waited a few more minutes to make sure it was all clear. Keeping Mia tucked close, she jogged around to Melindi's front gate. It swung back silently. How strange, it used to squeak. She had no idea if Melindi would be home or not, but she needed to speak to someone.

Yellow light spilled through the lounge curtains, casting a muted glow on the lawn. A shadow passed by, first one then another.

Bel's heart started thumping.

The first shadow was slight—Melindi. The second was much taller than her. A man's shadow.

She hasn't said anything about this to me. Why keep it a secret?

Bel crept closer. There was a gap in the curtains. If she could just get close enough…

Grateful for Mia's silence, she wedged herself between a large conifer and a rosebush. A thorn scratched her leg and she bit back a yelp. Warm blood trickled down. Ignoring the sting, she stretched to see.

Melindi was wearing a black dress which skimmed her curves and sparkled with diamantes as she moved. She flicked her hair back from her shoulders, laughing at something the man was saying. He moved closer, into view.

Ice ran through Isobel's veins.

It was Roric.

21

Back in her lounge with her doors locked, Bel eased Mia onto the couch and pulled a soft throw over her. It was past bedtime. Between that and her crying session, the little girl was completely worn out.

Bel stood in the dark, hugging herself to stop the trembling that rippled through her body like an aftershock. What now? She felt like a sleepwalker waking up to find the edge of a cliff at her feet. The solid ground beneath her had turned to quicksand.

Her desperate thoughts became prayers. *God, what now?*

Liam.

She had to phone him. She could only hope he'd understand. Working in the dark, she punched his number into her phone from memory. With each unanswered ring, her heart sank a little more. Her breath caught as he answered.

"Hi, this is Liam. You know what to do." A prolonged beep.

No! She whispered into the phone, "We're in trouble. You were right. About everything. I don't know what to do. If you are there, please pick up."

The upstairs floor creaked. She hung up, feeling perspiration break out on her forehead.

It's nothing, Bel. God, I can't stay here.

The walls that kept her feeling safe had dissipated like mist in a breeze. She was exposed, alone. She ran upstairs to pack for Mia, got half way up and stopped. There was no way Mia could stay downstairs by herself. She ran back to the lounge, thought about the extra weight and time lost and changed her mind.

Back upstairs. Mia's bag already had the essentials. Isobel threw in a few extra sets of clothing and a change of underwear for herself. A quick glance around the room. Nothing important.

Back downstairs. Mia's bag tugged on her shoulder like an extra toddler.

Relief washed through her at the sight of Mia. She was still here.

Bel reached down to pick her up, twisting her body sideways to keep her bag from swinging forwards and hitting Mia. Awkwardly, she slid the little girl into her arms.

Mia woke just enough to slip her arms around Bel's neck. She clung on like a monkey.

Bel froze before opening the door. She had to slip out quietly, unnoticed. She eased the latch down and pulled the door back a fraction. Nothing stirred outside in her yard or next door. She had to go now or she'd lose her nerve.

The door swung open and she grabbed it with one hand, clumsily holding onto Mia with the other. She pulled too hard and it shut with a bang. Her heart was in her throat as she locked the door and hurried to her car. She eased Mia into the baby car seat, and straightened up to listen. No movement.

She eased the driver's door open, got in, and released the handbrake. The car rolled backwards down the driveway, picking up momentum as it went. She reached the road, and the car changed direction to follow the slope. Past Melindi's house, she found second gear and roll-started the car. Years of having a dodgy battery were finally paying off.

It was time to find Liam.

****

Dr. Liam Brigham had found excuses to avoid going home all day. After getting off work, he'd wandered aimlessly through the biggest mall he could find, lingering in the bookshop. Maybe a good murder mystery would take his mind off everything. By the third back-page blurb full of blood and secrets, he felt dangerously close to throwing up. Not his brightest idea.

He found himself in a clothing store. He hated shopping for clothes, but he needed a few new T-shirts. On the way to menswear, he found himself stuck in the girls' section deliberating between getting a pink or purple fairy dress for Mia. At that, he left the shop and let his feet take over. It was no surprise to find himself in front of Isobel's house. All was in darkness. She was either fast asleep or out. He hurried on before she caught him outside. He didn't want to make her life trickier than it already was.

His feet led him to the beach and he walked along the water's edge for ages in the gloom. Each cold wave rushed around his ankles, receding with a hiss. Over and over, until the water no longer felt icy, but warm. Almost inviting.

He prayed as he walked. His conversation with his Father touched the patients he'd seen today, their broken bodies. He even prayed for sour Angie and he couldn't help grin in the dark as he asked for her to be filled with so much joy, she'd laugh in spite of herself.

As inevitably as the waves returned to his feet, he came back to the centre of his heart—Isobel and Mia.

God keep them safe. Watch over them and deliver them safely from their enemies. As the thought left his mind, he was struck with an urgency.

Go home, Liam. Go home now!

He changed direction, chiding himself for walking so far. With every step closer, his hurt grew heavier. He began to run. Feet pounding the pavement, he ran faster. Pain seared through him, his breath coming in short gasps. He rounded the corner to his home, expecting to see evidence of disaster. Nothing.

No flashing lights or cop cars. No smoke or fire. He doubled over at his front gate, slick with perspiration, gasping hard. *Jesus, what was that all about? The urgency, the panic?* He shook his head and released the gate catch. He was halfway up the path, stepping cautiously in the dark, when the feeling of being watched descended on him like a thick cloak. *What was it that Isobel always called him? Paranoid? She may well be right.*

"Liam?"

"Bel? Is that you?"

"I'm here."

Heat flooded his face. Questions assaulted him, but he ignored them. He found her huddled in a corner of the porch, squeezed in next to the potted palm with Mia curled up on her lap.

"Let's get you inside. Come."

"Take her." She held Mia away from her, enough for Liam to slip an arm around her slight body.

He lifted her off Isobel's lap and she hung limp on his shoulder. She turned her head into his neck, breathed in, and sighed contentedly, snuggling against him. Liam thought his heart might implode.

Once she was safely inside, tucked into the bed in his spare room, he went looking for Isobel.

She hadn't moved from her spot next to the palm.

"My leg has gone to sleep. I can't get up."

"I got you." Leaning in somewhat clumsily, he grabbed her hand and pulled her arm around his shoulders. Before she could object, his other arm slipped behind her knees and he lifted, bracing her weight against him. Stepping into the door, his foot snagged a step and he stumbled, almost sending them both flying.

Isobel shrieked and tucked her face into his neck, shaking.

"Whoops! I've got you."

She threw back her head, smothering giggles. No tears. This crazy woman was laughing! Somehow, between her pins and needles, giggling, and his aching back, they made it to the lounge where he dumped her on the couch.

"Coffee? No wait, how about some hot choc?"

"Please."

His hands shook as he went through the motions of getting mugs and filling them with steaming liquid. Normally he avoided sugar, but they could both do with some.

She never wanted to see him again, yet here she was. What had happened to change her mind?

His heart constricted, and half the sugar on the spoon missed the cup and landed on the countertop. By morning it would be overrun by ants. He left it right there and carried their drinks to the lounge.

Thick silence blanketed the room, broken only by deep, even breathing. A single lamp in the corner spilled gentle light over Isobel. Curled up on the couch, hands tucked under her chin, she was sleeping.

He set the mugs down, pulled the throw over her, and settled in the chair opposite her. *Why are you here, Isobel?*

After all she'd put him through, he should wake her up and make her talk. But his concern for her ran deeper than any need for answers. So he sat. Studying the soft curves of her face by lamplight, the deeper shadows below her eyes, wanting nothing more than to see her free.

Jesus, You hold the keys to her freedom. Her answers are in Your hands.

We need You.

****

Her eyes opened to see Liam sitting in a chair staring at her. Exhaustion fogged her senses and she lay still, wondering if she was still at home in bed and this was part of her dream lingering. The numbness in her back told her otherwise. Liam's couch was as bad as hers. Consciousness returned slowly, pulling back the curtains sleep had drawn on the events of the night before.

"What time is it?"

"Three AM. Three twenty-two AM, to be exact."

She pushed herself upright, sure that her hair was a tousled mess. "I'm sorry for doubting you."

"Its history, don't—"

"Shh! I'm trying to apologize."

"There is nothing to apologize for."

"I was so rude to you."

He scratched his chin and thought for a moment,

"You've got a point."

"Be nice!"

"Apology accepted. What's going on?"

"It happened just as the ladies said it would." She stopped dead as realisation dawned. She fixed her eyes on him, ready to read every twitch or stutter. "Did you put them up to it?"

"What?"

"That intervention or whatever they called it. You were behind that, weren't you?"

He brushed off her question as he would a mosquito. "So why are you here?"

"I panicked. I saw him playing me exactly as the ladies said he would. That was creepy, but I could cope with it. After he'd left, I was desperate to speak to someone. I didn't think I could come here, so I walked over to Melindi. Before I could knock, I saw two shadows—there were two people in the lounge. I crept closer to see. Liam, it was him. Roric was in Melindi's house. It was too much for me. I ran home, threw some clothes in a bag, and came straight here."

"I didn't see your car."

"I parked down at the shop and walked up. Just to be safe." She bit her lip. "Liam. Melindi…he's after her kids. What are we going to do?"

****

Liam checked his watch as he unlatched the gate to Melindi's property. Five AM. Either way, this was going to be awkward. He slipped up the path in the pre-dawn glow. Moving quickly, he rounded the garage and peered in through the small window. It was a tiny single garage, with Melindi's car parked inside. Back around to the front, he knocked three times on the door. Feeling conspicuous, he checked all around to make sure he was indeed alone and knocked again. No sound came from inside. He tried the door handle. It swung down easily and the door pulled away from him.

Unlocked. Not good.

Liam slipped inside. The entrance hall was swept and in order. He checked the lounge, kitchen—everything in place, nothing strange. Down the passage, he found a bedroom off to the left. Empty. The one on the right, the nursery, was empty too. He kept searching.

The main bedroom, he assumed, lay behind a closed door at the end of the passage. As a courtesy, he knocked twice but heard nothing and pushed his way inside.

Melindi lay curled on her side, dressed for a night out, clutching something in her hand. Smudged makeup and tears told tales of a not-so-happy ending. An empty champagne glass lay tipped on the carpet.

The doctor in him took over. His left hand slipped to her wrist to look for a pulse, his right pried her hand open. Painkillers. The kind he only prescribed after major surgery. The bottle was empty. Not good. Her skin was turning ashen before his eyes. He found a pulse. Too faint. She was fading.

****

"Lim house?"

"This is Liam's house, Mia." She brushed the soft curls away from Mia's face, still puffy with sleep. This little trouper could sleep anywhere, through anything.

"Where Lim?"

Well now, that is the question of the moment, isn't it just?

"He's coming soon." She'd heard nothing since he left at 5 AM. It was 8 AM and she could no longer fight the growing sense of doom. Unable to sit still and do nothing, she sifted through the ideas that began sprouting in her mind, most of which were either dangerous, impractical, or—in some cases—both.

Keys jingled in the front door, saving her from her own zeal.

Liam's face was grim.

Mia didn't notice. She ran to him and jumped.

He caught her in midair and swung her around before settling her on his hip.

She tucked her head under his chin, patting his chest happily, singing a song in gobble-de-gook.

"Melindi overdosed. She's in the hospital now. They pumped her stomach. She's going to make it."

"What! And her kids?"

"Bel, there was no one else in the house. I checked."

"Maybe they were hiding under the bed or something..."

Liam shook his head.

Bel's legs buckled under her, and she reached for the couch as she felt the blood drain from her face.

****

Mia hit the water and giggled as cold splashes found her face. A chubby finger pointed at the water around where she sat on the stairs. "Pool. Simmin' pool."

Liam sat on the tiles watching her with his feet on the step, water splashing around his ankles.

Isobel sat on the other side of the child.

They'd been back and forth for the last hour, neither of them willing to budge. Their argument had outlasted Mia's breakfast, a game of catch, and was carrying on well into her swim.

"Why are you being so stubborn about this, Liam? It's the only way to find Melindi's kids. I have to go home."

"No! Bel, give me some time. There is a better way. Trust me."

Mia patted the water, first with her left hand, then with her right. She sang to the rhythm of her smacks, "No, Bel! No, Bel! No! No!"

He caught Bel's eye over the top of her head. "You would risk"—he pointed to the little blonde imp who sat oblivious between them—"hmm?"

"She wouldn't be at risk because she'd be here with you."

"She's your ticket. Without her, you are of no value to him."

"I know."

Mia smacked too hard, splashing herself in the eye. She tried to rub, but wet hands made it all worse. With arms sticking out like a starfish, she sat helpless and started crying.

Bel lifted her out the water and wrapped her in one of Liam's fluffy turquoise towels. She held her close, patting her dry. "I can't help thinking—if I were Melindi, I would hope that somebody would do everything within their power to get them back. She can't right now. By the time she recovers, it will be too late. There is nothing she can do, but we can." Her gaze dropped to Mia then back to Liam's in defiance. "I can and I am going to."

He held her stare, not looking away but measuring up her courage against the fear he saw in her eyes. "I need to tell you something."

"Whatever you say will not change my mind."

"Hear me out. I have a friend in the police force. He's a detective. We've been working on the case together."

"What? Why didn't you tell me? Why didn't they take over from the start?"

"One of his guys…was involved."

"Was?"

"It's all sorted now." Liam bent down to tie his shoe, swallowing his sentence. It wasn't true. Nass was working on finding the corrupt policeman, but hadn't yet. Liam felt sick lying to Bel. Knowing how stubborn she was, would she leave if she knew the truth? "So we need to get you and Mia as far away as possible until we've landed this guy. I have an aunt in Cape Town. I'm going to book you a flight down to stay with her. It's the best solution."

Bel's forehead creased, taking it all in. "Why didn't you tell me?"

"Just trying to keep you both safe. As I'm doing now."

Bel said nothing and slowly started nodding in agreement. "OK. Cape Town. I'll go. For Mia's sake."

"Let's get you packed up and out of here safely. We'll need some backup."

22

It was the strangest craft class Bel had ever taught in Rochelle's studio. The ladies all had their magazines in front of them, tearing out pictures that appealed to them for a collage they'd be working on over the next few weeks.

Rochelle had been delighted but not surprised that Isobel wanted to come back to teach. She happily handed the ladies back without any questions.

Mia had stayed at Liam's house with his housekeeper for the morning. Thembi came in three times a week to save him from all things domestic. Thembi was a mom, and Mia had taken to her instantly, grinning at her and calling her Bi. "Thembi" was, after all, such a mouthful.

The craft ladies welcomed Isobel back with much squealing. None of them mentioned their last parting. They simply eased back into their light-hearted banter. Their reaction to Liam was another matter altogether.

He sneaked in after Rochelle had left, and his appearance was like Santa coming down the chimney just as the kids decided he didn't exist and they could eat the jolly old elf's milk and cookies.

Isobel didn't know that it was possible for a bunch of grown woman to look so guilty.

"When Liam said backup, I didn't think he meant you lot." Isobel eyed them all with one eyebrow lifted. "Though apparently, you are all quite creative with your schemes and plans."

Mischa shook her head coyly. "The intervention? Oh, honey, that was all Liam. He had it all planned, down to the last..." Her voice trailed off. "Why are you all staring at me?"

Isobel aimed her eyebrow at Liam, who had the good sense to blush a tiny bit.

"I just came up with the basic scheme. These ladies added all the finer touches. My part was really minor."

"I don't actually want to know! Let's bring them up to speed, shall we?"

Over the next half hour, they plotted and planned.

"Can you ladies see why Bel and Mia need to be watched over from a distance?" Liam stood up and stretched, easing the kinks out of his back from sitting too long. "We can't chance Roric suspecting anything and bolting."

A chorus of nods and yeses followed.

Isobel felt hope for the first time since that morning when Liam had walked through his door looking as if he'd been shot.

Isobel leaned on the table, closer to the ladies. "We'll need to move quickly. Jules, can you get hold of your friend at the newspaper about Melindi? That is first priority. Whoever is masterminding this, needs to believe that her 'suicide' was successful. A short article, no names mentioned, should do the trick. Ben's and Lilly's lives depend on it."

****

Less than twenty-four hours after her escape to Liam's house, Bel unlocked the door to her home. For all her bravado, faced with the cold reality of being there alone with Mia turned her stomach. *Calm down, Bel, you're only here long enough to pack.*

Liam had been called to the hospital for an emergency delivery. The mom was due in nine weeks time, but had arrived at the hospital haemorrhaging extensively. Liam suspected placental abruption.

Isobel insisted he see to his patient, waving aside his concern for her and Mia. Now? She was starting to think waiting would have been a better idea.

Mia ran straight to the basket of toys in the corner of the lounge and began unpacking, humming to herself.

Bel dumped her bag on the counter and rummaged inside for her mobile. Before leaving Rochelle's they'd created a group chat for easy communication. She sent two letters—HA—'home alone.' This tenuous connection to her craft ladies and Liam on the outside world was a lifeline.

Nothing had changed on the outside, but in truth nothing was the same.

Melindi was in hospital, fighting for her life.

Ben and Lilly were missing.

And here she was with Mia hoping to pack and leave before Roric showed up. She might as well slash her arm and go swimming in shark infested waters. *Let's pretend this is life as usual.*

Before she could pack anything, Mia needed food. It would be good for Isobel to eat something as well.

Omelettes seemed to be the quickest way of getting some nutrition into both of them. Isobel cracked eggs into a bowl and added milk. She was stirring in a pinch of salt when Mia came running in.

"Mine! Cum'see! Fowers!"

"Wait..." She just had time to turn off the stove

plate.

Mia gripped her pants in a death-grip and dragged her out the kitchen all the way to the lounge. In the middle of the coffee table sat a single orchid.

Bel loved flowers—cheerful daffodils that heralded spring, frank daisies with nothing to hide. Orchids? Just a little bit creepy. How did they get in the house? That was even more disturbing.

Mia was tapping the flower, watching it sway like a pendulum.

"Gentle, Mia." Her correction was out of habit, not concern for the orchid.

"Peppa!" Mia pulled a note out from between the stem and the leaves.

"Mia, let me see that."

"No." She was shaking her head, making her blonde hair swing. She clutched her prize to her chest, staring at Bel with wide-eyes. "No, mine."

The cogs were turning in Mia's brain, lighting her eyes with mischief. She held out the paper, snatched it away as Bel reached out, and ran. Her short legs were fast, but not fast enough.

Isobel caught up and grabbed her around the waist.

The little girl squirmed trying to get free, giggling and trying to keep her prize to herself.

On a different day, if the knot in her belly were smaller, Bel would have found the fun. With her ragged emotions kept under such tight control, this was nothing short of the perfect setup for a tantrum. Bel's heart sank; she ripped the card out of Mia's hand.

Mia siren-wailed on cue and the doorbell rang.

Bel flipped the card open and scanned for the sender.

The card held only a single, ornate R.

He'd been in her house.

She pushed the curtain back slightly—Roric's car was in the drive. *I'm not ready for this. God, I'm not ready for this.*

Mia was on the floor, taking out her displeasure on the carpet.

Isobel bent down to give her the card, but that window of opportunity had closed. She took the card, only to hurl it across the room and cry louder.

The doorbell rang again.

This was not how it was meant to happen.

Roric in her house, sitting on her couch… the flood of emotion buckled Isobel's knees.

Mia's tantrum was a blessing.

She hid behind it—justifiably angry and flustered.

He oozed charm and wisdom, but she knew the truth about him, and it had opened her eyes.

Once the storm of her temper had blown out, Mia took one look at Roric and retreated inside herself.

It broke Isobel's heart. "I'm just going to wash her face." Isobel picked up Mia and tucked her phone in her pocket on the way out the room. In the bathroom, she let the tap run and took out her phone. She needed her lifeline. *RH!*

With that sent, she wiped away Mia's tears. As her hands moved, her heart spilled through her lips.

Jesus, please…

****

"Doctor Brigham, the patient in C105 is awake."

"Thank you, Sister. Take over for me, please?" He handed her the syringe. "Buttock or thigh—patient's

164

choice."

By the time he got to Melindi, she looked ready to bolt. "What am I doing here? Where are my kids?"

"Your kids are...Isobel is...taking care of what they need right now."

Relieved, Melindi sank back into the pillows. "That's good. They love her. I feel awful. What's going on?"

"Do you remember anything? It would help us if you did."

Melindi went quiet. The heart rate monitor filled the silence with a constant stream of beeps. Slow and steady. Her eyes lost focus, brow furrowed with the effort of remembering.

Liam checked his watch, his mind going to the rounds that still waited for him before he finished his time. His mobile blipped as a text came through.

RH!

This couldn't be happening. He could do nothing. He punched his palm, willing it to be someone's face.

The beeping of the heart rate monitor shot up, double time. Melindi gasped. "It was him."

"Who? Melindi, tell me." Liam spun on his heel, back to her bedside.

"This guy I've been seeing. He gave me a pill. But it wasn't anything major, just something to help me relax. That's the last thing I remember. Doctor, what's going on?"

He needed to warn Isobel. "Excuse me for a moment." He left the ward typing a message. *Don't take any pills!* He hit send. The phone lost signal and the message didn't go through. Five times he hit send, and five times it failed. He had to get over there.

He nearly made it through reception when the call

came over the PA system. "Dr. Brigham, please report to casualty. Your immediate assistance is required."

He, who never swore, bit back a swear word and sprinted down the familiar passages. Casualty was carnage. A bus full of holiday-makers had lost its brakes and crashed through the street-side carnival. The walls were lined with injured, bleeding people and the promise of more on the way. The emergency medical crew had triaged and brought those in dire need of medical attention first, dealing with the lower grade injuries themselves onsite.

He paused long enough to type and send a single word.

Stuck.

****

Isobel sat on the couch next to Roric, close enough to feel the heat radiating from his leg alongside hers. Her hair was up in a ponytail but trailing wispy bits had escaped and hung softly in the curve of her neck.

Roric slipped a hand behind her head, twirling the stray hairs around his fingers.

Bel shivered in revulsion, but forced herself to stay put.

He must have mistaken her gesture to be one of enjoyment. He smiled. "You seem uptight."

"It's just"—her gaze strayed to Mia—"been a rough day."

He followed her glance. "Ah, yes. I understand. I can help, you know." His fingers traced circles up the side of her neck, with just enough pressure to untie knots and relax muscles.

If it had been anyone but him, Bel would have

turned to jelly. She got up to avoid his fingers on her skin. "I'll put the kettle on."

He followed her to the kitchen.

She filled a glass from a bottle of water in the fridge.

"Here, this will help." He dug in his back pocket and held out a capsule. It was half-pink and half-white.

"What is it?"

"Just a little something to take the edge off. It will help you relax."

"I don't think I need..."

Isobel watched as his eyes flashed with...was it suspicion?

Isobel gulped. Finding Melindi's kids might hinge on playing along. Or at least appearing to.

"Isobel?"

Her fingers trembled as she took the pill out of his palm. She'd been down this road before. She knew exactly what was coming. The capsule was different. The palm of the man offering it to her was too—but the intent was the same. It took every scrap of self-control to take it calmly and not scream at him.

She slipped the capsule into her mouth—not down her throat, but neatly under her tongue. Two great mouthfuls of water seemed enough to convince him she'd swallowed. At a guess, she had two minutes before the gel dissolved.

"There you go. You'll start feeling better soon."

Not wanting to risk talking, she smiled. Hanging on to her everything's-normal face by a thread, her emotions curled up tight inside—a screaming ball of fury and fear.

Mia was still engrossed in her toys. Her back faced firmly toward them, no doubt on purpose.

I am right there with you, my little girl.
Dear Jesus, Mia…

"I'll be back in a mo." She locked the bathroom door behind her, remembered Liam, and took the key out the lock and pocketed it. Opening the toilet, she ran water in the basin to cover the sound and spat the soggy pink and white mess out into the open loo. Just in time, she thought, by the bitter snap on her tongue. Everything inside of her wanted to curl up in a corner in never come out. This was too much to face.

She flushed, unlocked the door, and went downstairs. By the time she got to the lounge, her feet were tingling with a lameness that snaked up her legs.

That was some potent stuff in the capsule. Why was the couch spinning?

She sat heavily. Someone turned the light off in her head and soft blackness fell like a stage curtain on a final performance.

****

Liam stepped out of the booth to answer his phone. Kez-Lyn.

"Kez. What's up?"

Her voice was high, panicked. "I'm here with Sav, outside Bel's house. He's just left with Mia. She was either sleeping or drugged. No sign of Bel. What do we do? He's backing the car out of the drive. Liam?"

Liam's throat pulled tight. "Stick with him. We can't afford to lose Mia."

"What about Bel?"

"I'll get over there as soon as I can. Go now!"

The line went dead. His vision swam. Desperation tore through Liam. A room full of broken bodies stood between him and Bel's safety. Shutting down emotion, he became a machine. He stitched gashed flesh, bandaged wounds, and set broken limbs. He worked tirelessly, energized by the increasing urgency that pounded in his chest.

Bennett and Slade—the two doctors on call— arrived twenty minutes later.

Liam could have kissed them.

They fell into a rhythm and an hour after Roric had left Bel's house, Liam left the hospital.

He checked his phone. The last text he'd received from Kez had them southbound on the R102, fifty minutes ago. Nothing from Isobel.

God, what do I do?

He sent a quick broadcast to the group—*update please?* He punched in Isobel's number, then unlocked his car and got in while it rang unanswered. That was his starting point. He reversed out the car park and turned towards Isobel's house.

****

Heavy blackness clung to Isobel's eyelids, her mind. Far away, she could hear someone calling her. Liquid lead ran through her veins, making it impossible to sit up. Then out of nowhere, the feather-light touch of lips on her hers. Her eyes flew open. "Liam..."

He stood over her, framed by twinkling blackness at the edge of her vision. He grinned at her, though it seemed to stop short of his eyes. "I thought that would get you going."

Her lips were tingling furiously. With no energy to retaliate, all she could manage was a single eyebrow arch. It all came flooding back. Roric, the pill. Mia…

"Liam, he's got her!" Sitting took every scrap of effort. Sluggishness clung to her like sodden quicksand.

"I know."

"We have to go."

He didn't answer but leaned across, took something out of her hand, and studied it. An empty pill bottle.

What?

"Come. Moving will help get this out of your system." He slid in next to her, pulling her arm around his shoulders and slipping his arm around her waist.

"I didn't take those. He gave me something else. I spat it out. I think some of it got to me, though." She leaned heavily on Liam, her legs buckling under her.

He shook his head. "Same set up as Melindi. This guy is getting careless."

"Is Melindi…"

"She will be fine. Still in hospital. We haven't said anything about her kids yet. I'm having the contents of her stomach analyzed to check what he gave her."

"Who is tailing?" They had managed one lap around the lounge. Isobel could feel strength returning to her limbs.

"Kez and Savannah. Though it's been a while since I heard anything."

"So what do we do now? I should have been there. Mia…" Her voice broke.

He checked his mobile once more—still nothing. He took her cold hands in his warm ones. "Until we've heard from them, the only thing we can do is wait. Wait and pray."

They sat together for what seemed like an eternity

in the dark, not wanting to turn on the lights just in case Roric was nearby.

The long silence was broken only by the sound of a message arriving.

Liam opened it, paling at the words.

Lost them.

23

Isobel could tell by the Liam's face that the news was bad. "What now?"

He shook his head. "They lost the trail. We have no leads."

When he turned to Bel, she saw the pain in his eyes.

"Come. We are going to find them." He held out his hand and she put hers in it without a second thought.

They drove toward the edge of town, passing from inky blackness into the puddles of light thrown down by streetlights. The sea curved along the left of the road, a restless turning of waves crashing and retreating, each surge gaining ground on the expanse of bleached sand between them and the water.

Ten minutes into the drive, Isobel broke the silence. "Do you have a plan?"

He was quiet for so long, she thought he hadn't heard.

As she plucked up the courage to ask a second time, he spoke.

"We'll head in the direction that Kez and Savannah were going. We'll find them. After that? I don't know."

"Why? How can we just drive, not knowing where they are?"

"My heart tells me this is a good idea."

Bel could find no suitable answer to that, so she said nothing. The moon peeped over the horizon, casting sparkling light over the expanse of the water.

"I got the results of Melindi's stomach contents."

"Tell me."

"A potent cocktail of oxycontin and diphenhydramine."

"Which is? Rat poison?"

"No, that happens in movies. The capsule he gave her didn't come from the bottle he left in her hands, that's for sure. One is a narcotic used for pain, and the other is an antihistamine that is also used as a sedative. The dosages he mixed were off the charts. I think I got to Melindi just in time." He shot a glance at her and reached for her hand. "And you. Grief, Bel. I can't get my brain around the *what if.*"

Bel blanched at the thought of the bitter aftertaste on her tongue. Too close. It was enough to make her feel sick.

They drove the streets in silence.

Isobel fought rising panic with each minute that ticked past.

Streetlights gave way to tall trees, the forest thickening around them like an army closing rank. The road veered inland leaving the crashing hiss of waves behind them.

By the time they reached Kez and Savannah, Isobel was so tightly wound it felt as if her head might explode.

The two ladies rested on the bonnet of the car, pulled off the road beneath the sprawling umbrella of a coral tree, its fiery flowers glowing in the moonlight.

Savannah had her arm around Kez, who was weeping softly. No tears for Savannah, but she looked grim, as if every drop of life had been sucked out of her.

Bel got out the car.

Kez ran to her and threw her arms around her, whispering apologies nonstop. "It was all the cows' fault. They started crossing the road just as his car drove by. We were stuck. We couldn't risk driving until they were all well across the road. By that time, we'd lost sight of him. The road forks and splits, there are many turn-offs. They could be anywhere."

Savannah's phone rang. Checking it, she frowned. "It's Maggie." She moved away from the others to answer. They watched her expression cycle from grim to disbelief to wonder. By the time she ended the call, her face was beaming.

"That woman! She is something else."

Isobel tugged her arm. "What now? Spit it out."

"She couldn't sleep after your first message came through. So she tagged along. She picked us up along the R107, got a bit lost—which is why the cows didn't affect her."

"And…?" Isobel could scarcely breathe.

"Maggie is parked in the bushes outside the house Roric is in with all three kids. She wants to know where we are."

Liam grabbed Savannah by both shoulders. "How do we get there?"

"Follow me."

The two cars snaked through the quiet roads in the dark, headlights on dim. Less than ten minutes later, after a series of rights and lefts, they pulled up along the side of the road, as far into the bushes as their cars would fit.

Isobel found a path and would have been halfway

down it, but Liam caught her by the shirt.

"Wait, Bel," he whispered, "we need a plan."

"My baby..."

"Just one minute. Stay with me." He felt for her hand and held it in both of his. Under a living canopy of ancient trees too thick to let the moonlight through, they drew close, whispering in the stifling heat. "I've been thinking this through while we were driving. These people have influence in the police and social services. Who knows how far that influence spans? We need irrefutable, documented evidence if we are going to put an end to all this."

"But he has the kids. Surely —"

"He has Melindi's kids, but right now, because of the so-called suicide attempt, she's considered a mental patient. Her testimony..." He spoke to them all, but the gleam of his eyes sought out Bel's in the dark. "And we have no legal claim to Mia. I don't want it to be our word against theirs in a bought-off courtroom. It would be terrible if all the trauma you are going through now was for nothing." He squeezed her fingers and she nodded, blinking away hot tears.

He took a moment to collect his thoughts. "We need to be absolutely quiet. Leave your phones in the car. We cannot rescue them just yet. We'll split up and get in and out as quickly as we can. If you see them, don't let them see you. For now let's just make sure they're alive and together. Got it?"

The ladies nodded.

Liam waited for Bel to look him in the eye and agree before carrying on. "If you see Ben, let me know. I need him. Follow me." He fiddled with something in his pocket, then held a single finger to his lips. Using two forefingers, he indicated for them to get moving.

The house Maggie led them to was nestled in the woods a stiff hike away from the road. The path to the house was little more than a double dirt track, overgrown from years of disuse.

Walking through thick darkness, The silence pressed in on Bel. Her heartbeat seemed deafening in her own ears. He would surely hear her coming.

They walked in single file, eyes adjusting to the gloom with each step they took.

A dark figure stepped out of the shadows. Isobel bit her tongue to stop the shriek. Maggie. She put a hand to her lips and signaled them to follow her through an overgrown archway.

The garden surrounding the wooden house was overgrown with blackjacks competing with ivy in a tangled mess. Light blazed from the two windows along the front of the house. Paler light shone from those around the right side.

Isobel had been holding her emotions in, holding it all back for too long. She overtook Liam. Listening to her gut, she avoided the brightly lit front window and made straight for those down the right. Isobel found herself praying as she got closer to the window. With her back against the rough wood, she took a moment to calm herself before peeping in.

The curtains were open—or non-existent. Hard to tell from this angle. One window was slightly open, but thick burglar bars stopped any thought of quick rescue.

Isobel's eyes were still adjusting to the pale yellow light cast by the lamp when she heard Ben's voice. He was on a grubby blanket on the floor in the far corner of the room.

Lilly was on his lap, her head buried in his neck.

So still she could be sleeping.

Please God let her be sleeping.

His other arm was around Mia. The small girl was tucked in as close as she could get, arms around her drawn-up knees.

Every tiny part of Bel wanted to rip through these walls barehanded, scoop them up, and run.

She strained her ears to hear what he was saying.

"And that's why squirrels have such long tails. You can't buy umbrellas in the bush."

He was telling stories. Looking after the two girls in his life in a way that made Bel want to weep. They all looked tired, but Bel could see no obvious injuries.

Mia reached up and patted his cheek "Where mine?"

"Your what?"

"Mine. Want mine." Isobel could see the quiver in Mia's lip even from where she stood outside.

"Your mom?"

"Mine. Mine's mom."

"I'm sure she is on her way." He smiled a smile so gentle that Isobel fell apart. Tears streamed down her cheeks and she sobbed wordlessly. Great silent gasps.

"Sleep time, Mia." He eased his baby sister off his chest, carefully laying her down on the blanket. "Here, come sleep by Lilly. She needs you."

Mia nodded, gravely accepting her position as Lilly's helper.

With both girls down, Ben extricated himself and stood over them like a guardian angel, watching until the slow rise and fall of their chests spoke of sleep.

Isobel put a hand against the window and was about to get his attention when the sound of a door swinging open on its hinges broke the silence. She dropped down behind a bush. A sharp branch jabbed into her back and she bit back a scream as footsteps drew closer around the corner of the house.

From the silhouette it was Roric. He carried a torch, sending a bright beam of light carving through the shadows. Agonizing pain burned up and down her spine from the tip of the branch, but he was so close, she dare not move. She sank lower into the shadow, closed her eyes and dropped her head—willing him not to see her.

Gravel crunched as he came closer. Any moment, his hand would be on her neck. It would all be over.

The torchlight swooped an arc just below her and just above her. He turned away, muttering to himself.

Bel waited until she heard the front door before standing, moving away from the branch.

Liam poked his head around the corner and she pointed wordlessly toward the window.

Isobel shook with fear, a cocktail of hope and horror spiking her veins with adrenalin.

Liam moved alongside, panther-like. He gave the room a quick once-over and ducked to the side next to her. Squeezing her hand, he leaned forward and kissed her forehead. His confidence wrapped around her like a blanket.

She snuggled into it, bringing it close.

He pulled her toward himself, speaking a mere fraction above silent into her ear, "Call Ben over, make sure he stays silent."

Bracing herself, she folded the rawness into a small ball, the ragged ache that would push her over the edge of caution and risk them all. Turning back to the window, Ben had his back to her. She dare not risk calling or tapping, any noise in this silence would be disastrous.

How?

The gravel under her feet… reaching down, she scooped up a handful of tiny stones. Picking out one, she bounced it in her palm—getting used to the weight. Then she threw. It landed just short of Ben. Two more flew silently and the fourth hit him square in the back.

He spun around and saw her.

She shook her head, finger to her lip, and then beckoned him over.

He glanced at the door, back to her, and then crossed the floor quickly.

So much to ask, to say—none of it possible. So she touched fingers with him through the gap, smiling at him through the tears that had formed on her lashes.

Liam moved her aside gently and passed a note to Ben. He read wordlessly, squinting at the scrawl. He passed it back and nodded. Liam took the note, scrunched it into his pocket and passed a round disc, the size of a large cherry to Ben.

He took it, examining it in the gloom, before tucking it safely into the coin pocket on his shorts. His eyes lit up and he nodded once. Scared, but hopeful.

Liam mouthed wordlessly, "We'll be back." Taking Isobel's hand, he led her silently away from the house.

24

Moonlight broke through the clouds, touching the treetops with a pale glow.

Isobel shut herself into Liam's car with as little noise as she could.

An owl flew off, hooting its disapproval at having its hunting disturbed.

The others were still not back yet.

"What was that?" The hurricane of emotion she'd been hanging onto so tightly blew to the surface and came out as anger. At Liam. "That thing you gave Ben. What was it?"

"Calm down, Bel. It's a voice recorder with a built in tracking chip."

"How can I be calm? If Roric finds it—"

"We have to have evidence."

"He is an eight-year-old, Liam."

"He is a very gutsy, bright eight-year-old. Smart and resourceful."

"I don't know."

He didn't argue. He didn't rise to her anger. He simply took her in his arms and pulled her to his chest.

She stiffened.

He didn't budge. Leaning down, he kissed the top of her head. "You were very brave. I'm so proud of you."

Strangely, keeping him at a distance didn't seem so important anymore.

"So now what?" Isobel sipped the coffee in her hands, not wanting to drink it but knowing the caffeine would help her stay awake.

They sat in a lounge a mere stone's throw from where her heart lay sleeping on a dirty blanket. Back outside Roric's house, they had waited for minutes that took hours to pass. The other three emerged, shaken but unharmed.

Kez kept shaking her head and repeating over and over, "That was too close. Too close."

Maggie was a gem. More than that, she was turning out to be an entire treasure chest.

Liam had been quite willing to get together and discuss plans right there in the bush, but Maggie would have none of it.

A few calls later, they pulled up outside an empty house—a friend's holiday home. Maggie found the mains, the kettle, and soon they were nibbling on cookies and sipping hot drinks.

Isobel gave up on her coffee, setting it down on the side table. "I need to know the plan, Liam."

"I'm going to have to get back," Kez said. "My husband is going to grill me for sure."

Savannah drained her last sip. "Same here. Let us know what you need."

Isobel jumped up and hugged them each tight. "Don't have words to thank you."

"No need." Kez spoke and Savannah nodded.

Maggie left at the same time, fussing over whether they'd get by without milk.

Their car engines cut through the quiet, making Liam visibly cringe.

When he walked back into the lounge, Bel was waiting for him. "So what now?"

He checked his watch. "It's 9 PM now. Soon, we need to head back and keep an eye on the window. I told Ben to drop the recorder out the window as soon as he had something that would work as evidence. We need to be watching when he does that."

Bel nodded without comment. In her head, she had a parade of all the things that could go wrong. Giant holes in his planning that could see those kids slip through the cracks and vanish forever. "I'm ready to head back."

"I was going to ask if you thought we should take turns."

"If we are, then I want to go first." Isobel bounced on her toes, as twitchy as a gecko on desert sand.

"Well that's not going to happen."

"Then I guess we'll go together." Isobel smiled at him, sure that *try and stop me* was written all over her face.

Hours passed slowly. The pines needles that seemed such welcome cushioning when they'd arrived turned nasty, poking her with sharp green fingers.

Liam was next to her in the dark and with her senses heightened by no sight, she breathed him in with every breath she took. Time became meaningless.

Isobel began to feel like an astronaut adrift in space, suspended between two worlds yet unable to grasp either. Endless nothingness, just consuming concern for the young lives just beyond her reach.

****

The numbness in her arm woke her up. Dazed thoughts criss-crossed her brain, trying to break the surface to consciousness. Through the dappled shade of the trees, she could see the house. It lay tipped on its side. *How odd.*

Awareness came slowly. Her pillow was Liam's legs. His hand rested on her shoulder. She cringed. So much for that cup of coffee. She could only hope that she hadn't been snoring. Twisting her head, she could see that Liam hadn't even noticed that she'd woken up.

His eyes stayed fixed on the house, but his grip on her shoulder tightened.

Easing herself upright, she turned to see what had him transfixed.

Ben stood close to the window. He seemed agitated. Nervous. He took one last quick glance around the room, then shot his hand out the window, letting something drop.

Liam had stopped breathing.

"Do we get it now?" Isobel asked.

"It would be too easy to be spotted, but..." His forehead wrinkled in indecision. Resolution snapped across his face. He leaned in close, lips a mere breath from her ear, "I'm going to create a diversion out front. As soon as you've seen Roric leave the house, run. Pick up the recorder and make your way to the trees to the back. Don't make any contact with the kids just yet. Make sense?"

He moved away to see her nod. He pressed the car keys into her frozen hand and leaned in close. "When you have the device, take the car and get yourself to Maggie's cottage. Don't wait for me. I will find you." He pulled back and his eyes bored into hers, at once entreating and demanding she obey. He mouthed silently, "For the sake of those kids."

He melted silently through the trees.

Minutes later, a commotion broke out in the far

corner of the property. An explosion of weavers took flight, their bright yellow wings beating the air in displeasure.

If Bel didn't know better, she would have expected an elephant to come crashing through the hedge.

True to prediction, the door flew open and Roric ran out, gun in hand. He ran towards the source of the chaos, firearm ready.

Bel waited until his back was towards her as he ran away from where she hid.

Not sure if her jelly legs would hold her, she sprinted, ducking down by the flowerbed outside the window. Grappling around in the dirt, she came up with nothing but handfuls of soil. *It has to be here.* A shot shattered the morning quiet.

Not Liam.

Dear God, not Liam.

She took a deep breath, closed her eyes and opened them again. There it was! The recorder had snagged in the branches of a ragged conifer. She grabbed it and put it in her pocket. Everything was silent now. With no idea where Roric was, she gave herself no time to think. No time for fear. Holding her pocket closed, she ran for the cover of the trees, crashed to her knees, and felt the contents of her stomach rise. She swallowed hard, willing herself not to throw up.

Keeping Mia centre stage in her mind, she ran along the road, found the car, and turned back towards Maggie's cottage. Regret snapped at her heels as she drove. What if that shot hit Liam?

****

There was a split second between the clap of the shot and the searing fire across the top of his left arm. A jolt of adrenalin pumped through his veins. Biting back a low growl, he dropped down and lay still, panting in pain, clutching his wound with bloody fingers.

Roric crashed through the bush nearby. He swore and hit the bush with the gun in his hand. He turned back as quickly as he'd come, and all Liam could hope for was that his diversion had bought enough time for Isobel.

Not taking any chances, Liam remained dead still, not moving. A full five minutes later, he dragged himself to his feet.

Roric was nowhere to be seen.

Cradling his injured arm across his chest, Liam jogged towards where he'd parked. With each jolt, the pain shot through his body, setting stars to dance in his eyes. No vehicle in sight, so Isobel had managed to get away. He'd have to walk.

Perspiration and blood dripped from his shirt by the time he got to Maggie's cottage. His vision swam as he tried to aim himself at the one correct front door of the three dancing before his eyes. His blood-soaked hand slipped on the knob and he felt his knees give way from under him.

****

Isobel threw the door open and caught Liam. She staggered under his weight, but somehow kept her footing. They stumbled through the doorway. Isobel tripped and fell sideways, slamming her shoulder into the wall.

Liam came down hard, grunting as he landed on her and rolled to the floor.

Isobel got to her knees, dragged him inside and shut the door.

Liam struggled upright, his back against the wall. "Find bandages. Anything to stop blood flow. Need sugar water."

"Shh now. Save your strength."

She ran through the cottage, hunting in drawers and wardrobes for anything that could help. In the bedroom, she found a sewing kit with safety pins, needles and thread. A mirrored cupboard in the bathroom held a bottle of surgical spirits, a roll of toilet paper, and a hand towel.

By the time she got back with the kit, Liam was slipping down the wall, groaning in pain. She ripped off a thick wad of toilet paper, opened the bottle of spirits, and soaked the paper. The bullet had ripped through the thick flesh of Liam's deltoid, and it was bleeding profusely.

"I'm going to press this onto your wound, and keep it in place with a strip of towel and safety pins."

"Bel, stitch it."

"Uh-uh. Not gonna happen. I only brought that kit for the safety pins."

"There's no time. Disinfect the wound." Each word was an effort. "And the needle. It's like sewing a hem." He grinned, grimacing through the pain.

"You're making jokes, while I have to...sew you up like a hem. You are nuts." She rolled her eyes feeling heat rush to her cheeks. Being pushed into a corner seemed to bring out the worst in her. She focussed it all on Liam, if he hadn't got himself shot, she wouldn't have to put a needle through his skin.

Beneath that anger simmered a tangled mess of other emotions that she dare not investigate. Bel's anger was directed at Liam, but in truth, she was angry at Roric, at life, maybe even at God.

She threaded the needle and knotted the end, muttering under her breath. Pouring surgical spirits into a small plastic bowl, she curled the entire length of the thread and the needle into the liquid. She dipped a square of gauze, soaking it in the foul smelling fluid.

"Brace yourself." She mopped blood, applying pressure as she wiped.

Liam said nothing, but she could see the tendons in his neck bulge as he rode the waves of pain. Not stopping to think, she wiped her hands down with spirits, picked up the needle, and stitched the gash. It took twelve stitches. As she tied off the last knot, her belly heaved but she shoved the thought aside. No time for queasiness now.

"Good girl." He clutched the elbow of his stitched arm. "Now pad it and wrap it with a strip of towel."

Bel did as he said. "Done. That's as good as I'm going to get it." A wave of relief washed over her. The anger that had seen her through the makeshift surgery evaporated, leaving her cold and sick. She wrinkled her nose at his shirt. "You can't walk around like that."

Between them, they managed to slip off the soaked shirt.

"There's a spare in my car. I'll get it later. What did Ben record? Have you listened?"

She dug in her pocket and handed him the small device.

Clumsy with one hand not working right, he fumbled with the tiny buttons. He found play, and Roric's voice filled the air, pauses in between as he spoke on the phone.

"I have the merchandise…three of them, yes…no! I cannot wait. Deposit the money and I'll make arrangements to get them to you. It has to be today…their mothers are taken care of, no need for concern."

Liam and Bel stared at each other, partly in triumph but mostly sheer horror.

Bel recovered first. "I'm phoning the police. This has to be enough." The chair creaked as she pushed herself out of it.

Liam pulled himself upright. "Bel, wait!"

"What?"

"If you fetch my phone from the car, I'll get hold of the guy I've been working with."

Bel fetched his mobile and hovered over him while he dialled, her foot tapping.

He tried the detective's office first. It rang unanswered. His mobile went straight to voicemail. He tried both again and resorted to Nass's home line.

Nothing.

Each unanswered call threw sugar in the fizzy drink of Bel's impatience.

By the time he reached his fifth call, she left the room and dialled the local police herself.

25

"House is empty." Officer Ritchie, a burly, dark-haired man wearing a bulletproof vest and carrying a gun, jogged across the lawn to where Isobel and Liam were waiting by the cars.

"What? We were here forty-five minutes ago!" Isobel felt strength drain from her limbs.

Liam said nothing, but the muscles working in his jaw were a telltale sign of the storm inside.

"I'm sorry, ma'am. There is nobody home." He hung over forwards, red in the face and gasping for air.

"What can we do? Our kids—"

He unclipped his vest, lifting it off over his head. "Come down to the station. We'll open a case." The radio in his vehicle crackled to life. "Excuse me, I need to answer this."

Bel sought out Liam's eyes. She sent him a slight glance to the house and a brief head-tilt.

He nodded.

Officer Ritchie finished on the radio and called to them. "Follow me down to the station, folks. We'll take it from there." His movements were lazy, making Isobel wonder how much concern he had for their missing kids.

Liam offered a mock salute. "Yes, sir! We'll be right behind you." He sent a grim wink to Bel.

As soon as the squad car disappeared around the first corner, they ran to the house. The front door stood open. Neglect creaked through every squeaking floorboard, every rotten panel. The wooden porch pillars sported hundreds of tiny holes. Wood borer. Spider webs hung like moss in the corners, dusty trails blowing in the breeze.

"What made you phone that guy?" Liam asked.

"We needed to do something and your Detective Whatever-His-Name-Is was spectacularly absent. What was I supposed to do?" Bel eyed him sideways. "Why is it such a big deal anyway?"

Liam wiped a hand across his brow, shielding his eyes. He knew he shouldn't have lied to her about the traitor on the police force having been found. Now, his omission could cost the lives of the children. He opened his mouth to speak and then shut it again. There was no time. "It doesn't matter. Let's get hunting."

The cottage was small. They made their way to the back, to the room where the kids had been kept. The dirty blanket lay in the corner where it had been the night before. They scanned the room for anything that might give them a clue.

Liam shook his head. "I don't think we're going to find anything. I'm going to check outside the window."

Isobel hardly heard. Clinging to calm by a thread, she felt herself edging toward the brink. There was only so much she could cope with, and she was way beyond that point already. *Please God, if there is anything here... show us.*

She knelt down, putting her ear to the ground and getting her eye in line with the floor—an old trick her Grandpa had taught her to find lost things. Nothing. She scratched her head.

Liam called through the open window, "Nothing out here either. I guess it's time to head to the police station."

"Uh-huh." She hadn't heard a word. Her mind was turning over each part of the room, a giant puzzle that needed solving. She picked up the blanket to shake it out and fell to her knees. "Liam! Come quick!"

Within seconds, he ran back into the room. "What?"

"Look!"

There in the thick dust, traced by a shaky finger no bigger than Ben's, were three words: *fish and chips*. Both of the *s's* were written backwards.

"Was he hungry?" Bel said. "Or is it a message?"

Liam shook his head. "Poor boy must have been starving. I can't see that there's anything else to it."

"I'm not so sure, Liam. Maybe we should ask Melindi."

"You know what that means, don't you? If we want to ask her, we'll have to tell her they're missing."

Bel cringed. "I wish there were another way, but we're out of time. If he gets them off South African soil…"

Liam put an arm around her and drew her roughly to his chest. "I know. Let's not go there now. "

His kindness removed the lock she'd held carefully in place. All her emotion came bursting out like a cupboard stuffed too full of clothes. Bel wanted to scream, pound his chest with her fist, shake someone…instead, she pulled away from him, dashing tears from her cheeks. "I don't think Mia got her banana this morning. That thought is too much—"

"I know." He took his phone out of his pocket and snapped a photo of the words. "Let's go get them."

He was feeling it too and somehow that made it possible for Bel to breathe.

****

Melindi, dressed in a green hospital gown, was perched on the edge of her bed like a teenager at a prom waiting for someone to ask her to dance. She was happy to see Isobel, but even happier to see Liam.

"Doc, when can I go home? I want to see my kids."

There was no handbook on how to tell a friend that her children were stolen, no guidelines on the Internet. Of all the ugly things Isobel had lived through, this moment was shaping up to be right there with the worst of them.

Liam gave Melindi a quick once-over. He checked her pulse, briefly lifted her eyelids. "How are feeling?"

"Great. I want to go home."

"Melindi, listen to me. Roric poisoned you for a reason. His business is human trafficking. He was after your kids."

"What?"

"He intended for you to die so that he could take Ben and Lilly."

Melindi stared at him, face blank—uncomprehending. He could have been speaking Martian. Or ancient Swahili. As the words filtered through, sank in, and took hold, quiet fury blazed in her eyes. Her face contorted in desperation, disbelief. She got off the bed, trying to get past Bel and Liam, hospital gown or not. "Where are they? I want my kids. I want to go home. Now."

Liam caught her. "He's got them, but we are tracking him. We need your help."

"You let him take my kids!" She turned on Isobel, her eyes wild, accusing. "I trusted you! What kind of person are you?"

Liam tightened his grip. "This is not Isobel's fault."

Isobel stopped him with a hand on his arm. "It's fine. Mel, I haven't been completely honest with you. Mia is not my friend's child. I never knew her mom. Mia was the next in line to be kidnapped. We suspect Roric had something to do with her mom's disappearance. Liam brought Mia to me to keep her safe." Her voice caught in her throat, guilt thick and raw. "But I couldn't do that right either. He took her."

Melindi stared at her, mouth open.

"I found Mia abandoned on the beach. It seems he poisoned her mom just like you—but we suspect not with drugs in her body, but lies in her mind. They prey on single moms. Mess with their minds, convince them to commit suicide. If that doesn't work, they simply"— her tongue tripped over the words— "commit suicide for them."

"I don't believe you. What are you saying? You've been lying to me all along?"

"I didn't believe it at first either, but the fact is— Roric nearly succeeded with both of us. I never wanted to lie to you, Melindi. I just didn't know what else to do."

The silence hung between them like a vast ocean.

Melindi struggled to breathe, clawing her way to the surface through swimming doubts and aching fears.

Liam reached out and took her hand. "We need your help to figure out a clue that Ben left. We can't waste any time."

Melindi blinked, felt for the bed behind her, and sat. "I'm so sorry. I—"

Bel stepped closer. "I know what you're feeling."

Liam held out his phone with the picture. "Does this mean anything?"

"Did Ben write that? He can't get his s's right." Melindi clung to the phone as if it were Ben himself.

"Either he was hungry, or he might have left this as a clue. Any ideas?" Liam gently pried the phone out of her hands.

"There's a little shopping centre further down the coast. We drive out there sometimes to buy fish and chips. It's a treat. We used to do it when my husb…err, the kids' dad was still around. We haven't gone for ages. Ben loved it. "

Isobel frowned. "Fish and chips. Odd. Is there anything else there?"

"Oh, yes. It's a travel stop. From there you can get on the national bus route or take trains to anywhere in the country." She grimaced as she realized what she was saying.

Liam paled. "He's getting ready to move them. Bel, we need to get to that centre. Melindi, you can't come with us."

"You can't stop me. I'll tail you in a cab if I have to." She pulled her clothes out of the metal nightstand, reached down to get her pants over her feet.

Liam shut his eyes. "Listen, you shouldn't…" He sighed in resignation. "All right, fine. I'll sign you out. But you go to the police and open a case of kidnapping. If Isobel and I did it, it would take too much time. With every train and bus waiting—we have to get where he's going."

Melindi was torn. Stuck between her instincts and

logic—what a miserable place to be. "My stubbornness is costing precious time. Go. I'll do as you ask." She pressed scrawled directions into Isobel's hand. "Don't let Roric get away with this." A sob caught in her throat. "How could I have been so stupid?"

"Don't go there. I fell for him, too, remember?"

Liam shook his head. "I want to introduce his face to my fist." He signed at the bottom of the clipboard, tore a thin strip of paper off the edge of her sign-out form, and scrawled a name and number.

"You are free to leave, ma'am. Find Detective Nass. Speak to him only. Don't go to anyone else. Bel, give Melindi the recording from Ben."

"I gave it to Officer Ritchie. Nass can get it from him."

"You did what?"

"Officer Ritchie has it. Is that a problem?"

Liam breathed deep, shook his head. If sick were a colour, he'd be cycling rainbows.

"I thought they'd caught the traitor." Realization dawned on Bel. "You lied?"

"All I wanted was you and Mia as far away from all this as possible."

"So I probably just threw away our only evidence."

Liam knuckled his temples, eyes squeezed shut. "We need to find those kids. Melindi, tell Nass to pay careful attention to Officer Ritchie. And while you're at it? Get to praying."

26

The drive to Ben's fish and chips would have been a delight under any other circumstances. The road meandered lazily along the coast, a single lane that dipped and curved, sea on the left and graceful trees sharing their shade on the right.

"Question for you?" Bel shot a sideways glance toward the passenger seat. The telltale signs of sleeplessness had etched themselves into the creases of Liam's smile lines and the dark shadows under his eyes. He fidgeted nonstop, apparently not comfortable being driven.

He lifted his arm to test it, and flinched from pain. "Shoot." He checked the rear view as she overtook a slow-moving truck.

"Why? Why are you championing our cause? And please don't brush me off with lame excuses. Gut-level truth. Nothing less."

He shrugged as if it didn't really matter to him either way. "Your cause is my cause."

"No, that's not it."

"It is, actually." He shot her a glance that dared her to argue. "One of the babies stolen was mine." The way he said it was so matter-of-fact.

"That's not funny, Liam."

He kept staring straight ahead, focussed on the truck in front of them. Something in the set of his jaw said he was not joking.

"You're serious. I'm so sorry, Liam. How—"

"Courtney was my girlfriend for a few months. It just wasn't working. I broke it off, not knowing that she was expecting my baby. When she came to me with this tiny boy in her arms, it was a complete shock. I didn't have the luxury of nine months to get used to the idea. I decided it couldn't possibly be mine. I wasn't ready to take in some other man's baby with a woman that I couldn't live with." He turned the air conditioner on.

The sun had climbed the sky and was blazing down, heat rose in waves from the road ahead.

"But I decided to have the DNA test done, just to settle the issue. The day the results came back was the day I found her dead in her home. The baby was gone." Liam rubbed his tired eyes. "He'd be walking by now."

Bel had no words. Cold reality wrapped around her. "This is not right."

He reached over and she knew what was coming. Leaning across, he planted a kiss on her temple.

Finding fish and chips was a simple matter of hopscotching from neon sign to neon sign. A growing sense of dread had been building in Isobel with each passing minute. There was no more denying the facts.

Roric was a killer and he had Mia.

The last sign straddled the road, highlighting a turnoff to a parking lot buzzing with cars and people. The bus depot was off to the left behind a row of glass and metal booking offices. Each bus company had their own office, their signs competing for the business of the travelers.

Bel pulled into one of the few open spaces.

"Did he ever phone you?"

"Who, Roric? He did. Why?"

"Just wondering. Have you got your mobile on you?"

She checked her bag, a black miniature leather backpack. It was only just big enough for her phone, keys, wallet and a few tissues. "Right here."

"Good. Let's go."

Isobel got out of the car, and the heat washed over her like dragon's breath.

The place was a sprawling hive of buildings and people, covering many miles of ground. Finding Roric here would be impossible.

God, please.

Liam stretched out and took her hand. "Come. Let's start by finding that fish and chip shop."

"I don't know, Liam. Surely he won't take them out in public?"

"We have to start somewhere."

They inched their way through the thick press of people.

She clung to his fingers like a lifeline.

He pulled her close to him and tucked her in under his good arm as they walked. Leaning close, he whispered in her ear, "We can't let the girls see us yet. I don't know what Roric would do if they started making a scene. I don't trust him."

Bel froze, staring at a sign hanging overhead. "That makes perfect sense."

"Of course it does." He stopped too, frowning at the wonder on her face. "Wait...what are you talking about?"

She pointed, "Look! A roadhouse. Of course!"

"Good thinking, girl. He can get food without being in amongst people."

They ran through the narrow alley between shops. Vendors had set up makeshift stalls along the entire length of the walkway.

Bel dodged a kid on a rusty bike.

As they reached the other end, Liam pulled her flat against the wall.

The cars lined up in rows in front of them, waiters crisscrossing the hot tar, some carrying food, others taking orders to the kitchen.

Isobel spotted Roric's car. It was second from the front in the queue closest to them but at a wrong angle for her to see if the kids were with him.

"Bel, give me your phone."

She turned for Liam to dig it out of her backpack. Opening the logs folder, he found Roric's number and dialled. They watched his car as he leaned forward and picked up his phone.

"Who is this?" Roric asked.

Liam arm tightened around Bel's shoulders.

A pick-up truck pulled up to the drive-by, music pumping through the open windows.

Roric glanced at the truck, then at the phone in his hand.

Liam punched the end call button.

If Roric heard the music, he'd know they were close. Roric's car started and began pulling out of the parking.

A waiter with a tray full of food came out of the kitchen, saw him taking off, and jogged after him awkwardly, shouting.

Liam and Bel ran to keep up.

He drove across the complex towards the train station on the right.

Bel and Liam dodged cars, weaving through the

gaps. He was getting away.

Liam pulled Bel's hand. "Shortcut."

Taking the narrow path between the men's and ladies' ablution blocks, they cut diagonally across the centre, avoiding cars but not the people. They squeezed between the press of bodies, most of whom seemed to be going in the other direction.

They burst out of the tunnel to see Roric boarding a train. He had Lilly on his back in a baby carrier, a firm hand around the back of Ben's neck. Mia was clinging to Ben, who was carrying her clutched tight to his chest, her face buried in his neck.

Elastic shock shot through Isobel at the sight of her baby.

Ben stepped onto the train without seeing them, but Roric turned towards them. His face blanched at the sight of Isobel, shock replaced by quick fury. He drew back the jacket he was wearing. He gestured to the gun tucked into a holster around his body, likely the same gun that had ripped Liam's arm. He smiled at them, shaking his head as if to say, *don't follow me.*

My Mia! Every instinct drove Isobel forward, but Liam grabbed her round the waist and pulled her back.

"Wait, love, stay here."

Isobel fought his grip, turning to punch him.

He winced, face contorting in pain.

"Your arm! Oh grief, Liam. I'm so sorry. I can't take this."

He gasped through the pain. "We're getting on that train." He grabbed her hand with his good arm and they ran flat out across the hot tar.

They leapt into the last car, and the doors snapped shut behind them.

"Let Melindi know where we are." He sank onto

an open seat clutching his damaged arm, breathing heavily.

"Where is this train headed?"

"No idea." A wrinkled man dressed in an olive sweater sat in the next booth, squinting at a crossword puzzle. Liam leaned over and tapped him on the shoulder, "Excuse me, sir, where is this train going?"

The man let his pencil hover over his puzzle as he squinted up at Liam as if his head were vacant. "Up towards Johannesburg."

Isobel messaged Melindi and then sat next to Liam. "What now?"

"Should we go see if we can find them?"

"And then?"

"Stay one carriage back. Lie low. Keep an eye until they get off. We have to stay close." Liam eased himself upright and together they crossed the carriage, staggering a little with the jerky pull of the train. They didn't pay too much attention to the one they were in, moving through to the next.

Nothing.

With each added carriage that came up empty, the tension grew.

"Has to be this one, surely?" Isobel couldn't take much more of this. She searched Liam's eyes for reassurance. What she got was a kiss on the forehead. She swatted him away, feigning irritation. The truth was, his stolen kiss tickled something deep inside of her. There was no logic in why that should make her feel better, but it did.

The next carriage was not the one either. They kept going and each time came up empty handed. By the time they reached the first carriage—the one directly linked to the engine—they knew Roric had tricked them. They were on a train following him to Jo'burg, except that he was no longer on the train. He'd probably boarded the train, walked through to the other side, and climbed straight off.

Roric was gone. And he'd taken Ben, Lilly, and Mia with him.

27

Isobel curled herself into the corner of the swing on her patio. She'd been there since before the birds stretched, yawned, and warmed up their vocal cords to herald the appearance of the sun. She stared out over the storm-tossed waves, not absorbing what she was seeing. Maybe if she could make herself small enough, she would simply cease to exist. She'd come into this town broken and bereft, and she would be leaving it in the same way. Dead or alive. It made no difference. Her heart broke with worry over Mia, Lilly, and Ben.

No hope. No hope. No hope. The mantra played through her mind on a continuous loop.

Melindi was home. But she kept her distance, probably grieving in her own private hell. There was nothing to say to her. Words of consolation fell far short of any real comfort.

It had been a week since they lost contact with Roric. Lost their only lead. Her mind kept returning to that day, gnawing on it like a famished hound. They'd left the train and headed back at the first station they'd stopped at, but it cost them an hour. In that hour, Roric had disappeared. No leads, no trail to follow. Maybe if they had done something different, the three would be home now.

Liam made food that Isobel didn't eat. He brought her blankets when the wind grew chill, only to leave them at her feet.

She slept in fits and start, never in her bed, just passing out on the couch or on the swing.

It was nearly midnight on Friday and she hadn't gone in yet.

Liam joined her on the swing.

All her silent musing distilled into one question. A question she'd been too scared to think, too afraid to ask. All the fragile threads that held life sacred seemed caught up in the answer...yet she was in the dark once again, considering the hand life had dealt her. There was no getting away from it any longer. "Where is God in all this?"

Liam pushed off and got the swing moving. "What do you think?"

"He is punishing me."

"For what?"

"More than I can count, I guess."

"Pick one."

"Having an affair. That was pretty stupid. Stupid and wrong."

"He's not punishing you."

She curled her legs closer to her body, vacant eyes taking in nothing.

"Oh, Bel, think of it this way. What is the worst thing Mia could do? Even if she did that very thing, would you ever put her through heartache like this? To teach her a lesson. Would you?"

She squeezed her eyes tight against the tears.

"It isn't His heart."

"Then what? It makes no sense. All I've ever known is betrayal. Loss. Any brief happiness turned out to be a setup for more hurt."

He moved closer, trying to pull her into his arms.

She stiffened and pulled away.

"Isobel, I don't have the answers to your questions. The only thing I have left is to trust what I hope is true. Somehow, in all this mess, He is good. We can't see it now, but it's a fact that cannot change." He fell silent. When he spoke, it was in a harsh whisper. "If I stop believing that, I have nothing."

He reached out for her, and she let him. He took her hand. He walked her upstairs and tucked her in bed, complete with the kiss on her forehead. By the time his lips left her skin, she was asleep.

*****

Liam was up before the sun. His body had still not adapted to Isobel's couch. Stretching to ease the stiffness from his spine, he put the kettle on for coffee. He didn't want coffee, but sticking to his habits brought some sense of normal. *Who am I kidding?*

The shower went on upstairs, and ten minutes later he heard the click of the lock in the door at the top of the stairs. Isobel came down. Her damp hair was brushed and shiny. Her clothes hung on her—not eating will do that to one—but they were clean and ironed. She came straight over and wrapped him in a hug. "I'm sorry, Liam. I've been so consumed in my own grief, I forgot that you've been doing this for months already. What you said about Mia, about me punishing her—"

The doorbell rang. Liam gave her a squeeze and went to answer it. "Hold that thought."

It was Melindi. She was pale. Haunted. "I've just had a call from the police. We have to get down to the station now."

28

Isobel didn't trust herself to drive. She handed the keys to Liam, he took them without a word. His arm was well on its way to recovery. He stuck stubbornly to the theory that it was Bel's good patch-up job. She shook her head and blamed the passing of time.

Melindi broke the silence. "The officer who phoned wouldn't give me details. I don't know what we'll find."

Hope and despair duelled viciously inside of Bel.

Liam voice-dialled Detective Nass. No answer.

Isobel sighed. Why the detective even had a mobile was beyond her. She found herself praying. If Jesus were standing in front of her, she would be on her knees with her arms wrapped around his legs. *If You truly are good and kind…*

They pulled to a stop outside the station and climbed out the car.

Isobel didn't know whether to rush or hang back in case it was bad news.

Melindi reached out and found Isobel's hand.

Warm sunshine glowed bright around them, urging Isobel to hope. She hung on to Melindi, grateful for the silent camaraderie.

Liam took her other hand. Together, they mounted the chipped concrete stairs and pushed back the glass panelled door to the police station.

The officer at reception had her hair scraped back

into a bun a ballerina would be proud of.

Liam squeezed Bel's hand and asked, "Where can we find Detective Brent? He called us in to see him."

"You're here about the kidnapping? Straight down the passage, left at the end, first office on the right. I'll warn him you're coming."

Bel searched the woman's face for a hint of what they were in for, a clue for her trembling heart. Nothing. Trepidation grew with every hollow step. Bel's hands started to shake.

Detective Brent was waiting for them outside his office. By the roundness of his face, he'd long since given up on lettuce. His expression was grim.

"Come inside, please." He followed them in and shut the door. "Mrs. Marais?" He glanced between Melindi and Bel, eyebrow raised questioningly.

"That's me, Detective. I'm the one who opened the case." Melindi had her hands firmly clasped.

Bel tried it, too, and it seemed to help the shaking.

"And these are?"

Melindi spoke for them. "Isobel Carter, Mia's mom. And Dr. Liam Brigham, her partner."

Elastic truth.

On cue, Liam reached out and took Bel's hand in his.

"Aah, Dr. Brigham, Nass mentioned you." He caught Liam's gaze for a brief moment. Apparently satisfied, Brent sat down and pulled the case file from the top of the tray on his desk. He left it there untouched. "I'm afraid I have some bad news."

Bel sank into the closest chair.

Melindi drew a shuddering breath and clasped the back of a chair, her knuckles white.

"Roric MacAllister is an alias. Greg Smethers is his

real name, and we've pieced together enough information to link him to a number of other crimes involving minors. The problem is he is still MIA."

Liam groaned, knuckling his forehead, muscles in his arms bunched as if he were about to hit something.

The chair squeaked under the heavy detective. "But I do have something else for you."

Bel buried her face in her hands, one eye peeping through a gap between her fingers.

"Officer Ritchie is currently under investigation. It appears that he has been deeply involved with the cases connected to yours. Suicides, missing children. We've found evidence in his home to suggest he was the one who recruited someone to pose as the social worker who took possession of each child. We are closing in on her, too."

Bel stared at him through her fingers, hearing words that didn't settle into coherent sentences. Her insides bled, shredded by a missing tiny person.

Liam hovered on the edge of the chair, tightly wound. "And our evidence?"

"Nowhere to be found. He probably flushed it." Brent regarded each one, compassion softening his face. "We also...have something for you." A smidgen of delight lit deep in his eyes. Nothing else shifted in his expression.

The knot in Isobel's gut tightened. *Mia? Could it be? Dead or alive?* She sat forward. "Our kids? Where? Are they OK? When can we see them?"

"They will be brought down soon. They're at Medical."

Melindi shot to her feet. "Are they hurt?"

"That's what they're assessing. Please sit down, Mrs. Marais. We'll get to all your questions."

"Detective, how did you find them?" Liam asked.

"Walked into the station. Said they were dropped off outside. The boy knew his mom's number, so we could phone." He shrugged. "It's a mystery."

"But that doesn't make sense." Isobel eyed the detective as if he were a street magician who had lost her diamond down his sleeve.

Interrupted by a knock on the door, Bel turned.

Ben came in first, subdued until he saw his mom. He ran to her, knocking an empty chair over in his rush. He buried himself in her arms. The bravery that had cocooned Mia and Lilly dissolved and he sobbed silently.

A nursing sister came in with Lilly on her hip. Her other hand held Mia's. The tiny blonde stood wrapped in silence, eyes on the tiles.

Isobel fell out of her chair and, like breathing air for the first time, scooped the little girl up and pressed her close.

Her blonde hair a tattered mess of knots, Mia tucked her head under Isobel's chin. Her arms hung limp, no tears, no smiles. But she was alive.

Ben stepped back as the nurse brought Lilly and placed her on Melindi's lap.

Melinda wept and laughed as Lilly bounced, patting her mom's cheeks.

Ben stood against the wall, dazed — dreamlike.

Mia wiggled out of Bel's arms. She went over and stood next to him, forehead pressed against his shoulder, as close as she could get. He put an arm around her. Crouching down, he whispered in her ear, "Mia, it's Mine. She's really here. Come." As tenderly as if he were holding a fragile snowflake in his warm hands, he shuffled on his knees, drawing Mia back to

Isobel.

Isobel ached for the pain she'd caused Mia. More than anything, she wanted to absorb every hurt, the crushing weight of abandonment. She got on her knees.

Ben put one arm around Isobel's shoulders, and with the other, gently drew Mia into Bel's arms. He extricated himself from the embrace.

Bel clung to Mia, pouring her heart out in whispers into her matted hair. "I know it felt like I left you. I didn't. When everything was dark around you, you were always on my mind. My love for you kept me hoping, kept me alive. I wish you could see into my heart."In her spirit, in her own words, she heard the echo of God speaking...

I know you felt like I left you. I didn't. When everything was dark around you, you were always on My mind. My love for you kept Me hoping, killed Me, and brought Me back to life. I wish you could see into My heart.

****

Steam fogged up the bathroom mirror and curled up in lazy twists from the bath. Bel rubbed conditioner into Mia's tangles. She began brushing out the knots with a wide-tooth comb, working with small sections at a time. Mia swatted the water, not interested in what Bel was doing behind her back.

Bel had run the bath too hot, then had to cool it so as not to sting Mia's nappy rash.

Roric had apparently barely changed her at all, and it would take serious mothering to get rid of the angry redness.

The comb snagged in an ugly knot. Mia pulled

away from Bel. "Ow! Stopit. No!"

Not prepared to fight on Mia's first day back, Bell put down the comb and rinsed the conditioner out, ignoring the knots. She picked up the soap and lathered the little girl's body, all the while looking for signs of trauma. Mia had never carried much extra body fat, but she had now lost it all. Her ribs showed clearly through her translucent skin.

He hadn't bothered to feed them too often, either.

Lifting Mia out the water, Isobel wrapped her in a soft towel and carried her through to the room. She rubbed lotion into the child's dry skin. The nappy rash cream made Mia cry, but Isobel persevered, knowing that it was the only way to make it better.

She carried Mia back to the bathroom and cuddled her in her arms to brush the child's teeth.

Mia fussed against her, wriggling to get away.

Bel spoke soothing words, but held her firmly and kept going until all the past week's build-up was gone. Getting her to sit still through having her hair brushed was almost impossible. Digging in her bag, Isobel found Mia's favourite dog-eared book starring a baby polar bear. It was a touch-and-feel book. Losing herself in the feel of soft polar fur and rough gravel, Mia stayed still long enough for Bel to finish detangling her fine hair. Bel kissed the top of her head.

Mia had withdrawn inside herself again. Few words made it past her lips and her eyes wouldn't meet Bel's.

A knock sounded on the door. "Safe to come in?" Liam called.

"Yep. Mia, Lim's here."

The little girl crawled onto Bel's lap and hid her face in her neck.

Liam perched himself on the edge of the bed. "How are things looking?" His tone was light and upbeat, but he gestured towards Mia with concern in his eyes.

"The nappy rash is ugly, but everything else seems untouched. The heart will take time to mend."

"How are you holding up?"

She pulled Mia closer and shook her head. "I don't know. Nothing is resolved. I'm back in limbo. Skating on a pond with ice that could crack beneath my feet."

Liam sat on the edge of her bed. "I'm sure it feels like that." He sighed. "I just wish you could see yourself through Jesus's eyes. He has good things for you. You can believe it."

"I don't buy it. Not anymore. I thought I heard from Him on the beach that night, and look what happened. He said the darkness was over, but it all got worse. Much, much worse."

Mia stirred on her lap. "Jesus!" She turned to Liam and her face crinkled in a smile.

"Yes, Mia. Jesus." Liam grinned back, damp collecting in the corner of his eyes.

She repeated it again, clapping with delight. It was the first thing she'd said all day. Apart from her moans at having her knots taken out—which didn't really count. Retreating inside herself again, Mia snuggled into Isobel's arms, resting her head on Bel's chest. A sigh shuddered through her body, but not a hopeless sigh. A sigh of contentment.

"Isobel, listen. Promises are given as light. What good is a blazing torch when the sun is up? You need that torch at night. When everything around you seems to be shattering, you can trust God's promises. Once He says something, you can believe it no matter what hits you. This whole thing, this mess…it will resolve. You'll see. You just can't give up right now."

Mia had grown too still. Sleep had crept over her.

Bel slipped the child down off her chest and into her lap. Soft hair fanned over Bel's arm like spun gold.

Liam was watching her with an expression in his eyes so tender, she could not put a name to it.

She looked away. "So what now? None of it makes sense. Why steal them and not go through with it?"

"I'm as baffled as you, but I know someone who might shed some light."

29

Ben was already tucked up in his mom's bed. According to Melindi, he'd eaten two helpings of dinner and had asked for more food. He was working his way through a bowl of cereal when Liam found him.

"Hey, big guy. How are you?" Liam pulled the corner of the duvet straight and sat on the edge of the bed.

Ben didn't reply but attempted a smile.

"You did a brilliant job recording."

The smile on Ben's face softened, becoming genuine.

"Do you mind if I ask you some things?"

Ben shrugged.

Liam took it as a yes. "What happened to the man who took you? Why did he take you to the police station and leave you there?"

"I dunno." Ben looked at him as if he'd crawled out from a cave.

"Was he cross? Scared maybe?"

"Nah, more like...confused. I think Mia did something to him."

"Mia? How so?"

"She cast a spell on him." He nodded sagely. Obvious.

Liam barked out a laugh but cut it short by clenching his tongue between his teeth. Ben's face was so sincere. "Describe it for me."

"This morning, Mia was crying. I think she was hungry. There were some other people coming and he was so cross. Anyway. So suddenly, Mia stopped crying, just like that. It looked like she was listening." Ben glanced around the room, leaned toward Liam, and spoke in a secrets voice. "It was so freaky. She laughed, nodded, and then walked over to him. I tried to hold her, but she got away. She went straight up to him, staring like he was a monkey in a zoo. I thought he was going to smack her. Then she climbed onto his lap, put her hands on his cheeks, and kissed him."

"What did he do?"

"He looked so confused. It made me want to laugh. After that, he took us to the police."

Liam frowned. "So Mia didn't say anything to him? Anything at all?"

"Nope."

"And she didn't say anything to you?"

Ben shook his head. He fiddled with the duvet, scrunching it between his fingers, and then smoothing it out again. "What if he comes back?"

"I am going to do everything I can to make sure that he doesn't."

Ben regarded him with tired eyes, as if he was weighing Liam up, considering him worthy of his words. Apparently, something in Liam satisfied Ben's need for reassurance. He sank back onto the pillows with a deep sigh.

Minutes later, Liam let himself into Bel's house with her spare key. He stopped for a moment, door in hand, struck by the realization that he no longer thought of himself as a visitor. *It's as if I belong here.* He savoured the feeling and for a brief moment allowed his head to wander the paths his heart had already worn bare. This was the real deal.

He shut the door behind himself and called out, "Bel! Where are you?" No answer. He hung his keys on the hook in the passage and climbed the stairs two at a time.

Bel was in the bedroom, packing clothes into a suitcase. For every five items she managed to put in, Mia would unpack one or two. Frustration bubbled close to the surface, blushing Bel's cheeks.

"You're running."

"How perceptive of you." She snatched a purple top out of Mia's hands and threw it into the suitcase.

"Don't do it."

"You have no right to demand that of me." She retrieved the purple top from Mia for a second time, folded her arms across her chest and glared at him. The top dangled from her armpit. Mia toddled over and tried to pull it down, giggling.

"When I left, we were good. Now, you are fed up with me. Why?"

Isobel tugged on the other end of the purple top. Tug-o-war with a two-year-old. She gave up and sank to the floor, running her hands through her hair. "I don't want to talk about it."

"Don't you want to hear what Ben had to say?"

Mia dropped the purple top, losing interest as Bel was no longer attached to the other end. She toddled over to Liam, craning her neck to stare up at him. She hugged his legs and said, "Ben."

He leaned over and gently ruffled her hair.

Bel clenched her jaw. "I just got all the knots out of that."

He ignored her comment, waiting for her answer.

"It won't make any difference. Nothing he said could change anything."

"Just give me some time. I'm going back to the police now. Just don't do anything yet. Please?"

****

Bel hooked Melindi's gate closed, pinching her finger on the wire holding it in place. She popped her finger in her mouth to take away the sting and thought how much she would miss her neighbour.

There was no doubt in Bel's mind now, she had to leave. There was no other choice. Seeing a red pickup drive past her house had sent any shred of security crashing. Roric—or whatever his name was—was back and intent on finishing what he'd started. The whole darkness-and-light thing on the beach was nothing more than wishful thinking. Roric was dangerous, even more so now that he'd let his catch slip through his clutches. He may have let them go once, but it was only a matter of time before regret set in. He would be back, twice as determined. Liam had been right all along.

Mia had tucked herself next to Ben were he sat playing a racing game on the PC. She squeezed in behind him on the chair and lay her head on his back. He was her knight, and nothing would change that.

Isobel had forgone Melindi's offer of tea to get back to packing, determined to make the most of her Mia-free time. She started up the path, looked up, and stopped.

The front door stood slightly ajar.

I could have sworn I closed it.

She ducked behind a bushy bottle-brush next to

the path. What now?

Liam would know what to do.

She shoved that idea aside. The whole point of this was to figure out how to make it on her own. Creeping forward, trying to avoid fallen, dry leaves that would give her away, she sneaked closer to the open door. Crossing the yard took an eternity. She made it to the porch and peered through the lacy lounge curtains. No movement.

Isobel stayed at the window, straining for a clue of who could be inside. Nothing stirred, and she began to feel a bit silly. If there were a shortcut to ridding herself of this paranoia, she would happily throw money at whoever could make it happen.

She hung around outside getting more and more irritated with herself. This was ridiculous. A grown woman spooked by a door she probably left open. That same door stood between her and the rest of her packing. Nonsense.

Squaring her shoulders, she climbed the stairs and pushed her way inside. Her head snapped back, and she felt sharp steel at her throat. Her scalp burned from fingers in her hair, and she tried to swallow. Every breath filled her nostrils with the familiar musky scent of aftershave. Roric.

Kicking the door closed, he dragged her to the lounge. She struggled to stay on her feet, swinging between the fire blazing in her scalp and the blade at her throat. Isobel wanted to scream. Her mind darted like a firefly. Any sound and he'd slit her throat. Phone was out of reach. She was out of options.

Jesus, please.

"Where's the kid?"

"Gone."

He tugged hard. Bel ground her teeth.

"Don't push me. Where is she?"

She forced words out, grimacing. "Not here. Found another home."

He ran the edge of his knife across her skin. Liquid warmth trailed down her neck. "Not good enough."

"She's gone. Give it up. Move on." Swallowing sent pain searing down her throat.

"Do not lie to me!" Every word a tug on her hair.

Her vision began to blur, edges fuzzy with throbbing agony. In the middle of it all, she saw Mia. In a moment of sharp clarity, she knew that nothing mattered to her more than the little girl's life. If she existed to keep Mia alive, that would be enough.

She heard the front gate swing open, and Mia's excited babble filtered through the open window.

Melindi responded.

Bel couldn't hear the words, but she felt the knife tip press hard against her skin. Any noise and he'd drive the point deep, ripping her windpipe. Calling out a warning would do no good. Her insides writhed in helpless desperation.

Someone knocked on the front door. The squeak of the knob turning. Tiny footsteps padded down the passage.

"Mine?" Mia called out. She burst into the lounge as if she were the seeker in hide-and-seek. She bounced in and stopped, eyes-wide at the sight of Roric and Isobel.

The pressure on Bel's skin increased a fraction, just enough to warn her.

Melindi came round the corner. Her face blanched.

Roric laughed, sick and slow. "Aaah. Just who I was hoping to see."

Melindi pulled Mia close, arm around her protectively. She drew back.

Roric shook his head, gesturing to the knife at Bel's throat. "Uh-uh. Stay put."

Mia stared at Bel. She'd picked up on the mood in the room; fear clouded her eyes. She fell quiet and turned her head to the side as a bird would, listening. Nodding, she smiled. All the fear in her face disappeared, as if someone flipped a switch. With a chuckle, she ducked under Melindi's arm. Before Melindi could grab her, Mia toddled straight towards Roric, her face alight with what could most closely be described as love.

Bel felt the blade quiver against her skin. Roric's grip in her hair tightened as Mia came close.

Mia wrapped her arms around his leg, upturned face beaming affection.

The knife slipped out of Roric's hand and fell with a dull thud on the carpet.

As his other hand released, Bel dropped to her knees, her scalp stinging. For a brief moment, she saw stars. Clutching her neck, she looked up to see Roric cringing away from Mia.

Mia had her arms wrapped firmly around his knees, cooing adoration.

Bel wanted to scream. Grab her baby. Run. But the longer Mia held Roric, the soggier he became.

Melindi ducked back into the passage, and Isobel heard her punching numbers into the phone.

Instincts burned inside Isobel. Snatch Mia and run. She forced herself to stand still. What she was seeing made no sense.

Roric was on his knees with Mia brushing her fingers through his hair. She jabbered non-stop, pausing only to put her arms around his neck and hug him tight. There were no recognisable words in what she said. She chattered on and he knelt as one hypnotised.

Isobel stood, one hand clutched her bleeding neck while her insides coiled tight, waiting for Roric to snap. She eyed the knife on the floor. Should she pick it up?

The crunch of tyres sounded on the paving.

Three men in blue uniforms came in through the open door with their weapons in hand. Roric put up no fight as they cuffed him, read him his rights and took him away. One of the officers bagged the knife, still covered in Isobel's blood. Through it all, Roric's eyes never left Mia's face.

She dimpled a smile and waved to him as he left.

Halfway down the path, he surfaced from the his daze and realized what was happening. He started swearing and threatening to hit the police officers who were arresting him.

Only when the police cars engines were out of earshot did Bel start breathing again. She dropped down to her knees, and Mia folded herself into Bel's arms.

Melindi wrapped them both in a clumsy hug from behind, breathing over them. "It is over. It's really over."

30

Isobel watched Liam take a third slice of pizza, wrapping the stringy cheese around it using his pinky. He bit into it, sighing happy contentment.

Ben picked out two slices loaded with the most bacon. He bit into one of them. "I like this picnic party." His words came out funny, spoken over and around the food in his mouth.

Isobel laughed. She pulled the picnic blanket straight. The rain outside had forced them indoors, but it could have been on an exotic beach somewhere for the joy inside her. It felt good to be happy. Glancing across the room filled with the people she'd come to love most, she found herself agreeing with God. Light had truly triumphed over darkness. With Roric gone, a black cloud had dissipated over the two little families.

This picnic party—on the floor of her lounge—was their celebration.

Liam gazed at her.

A blush crept into her cheeks and she fussed over the chip bowl, avoiding meeting his eyes. Her heart cautiously delighted in his attention.

Mia toddled around, picking her lunch off everyone else's plates. Pineapple from Liam, a cocktail sausage from Ben, she made her way around the circle moving on only when she'd chewed and swallowed. Each stolen morsel acknowledged with a sincere "Tank yooo!" gathering a fresh round of *aahs*.

They sat in the glow of Light that sent darkness crashing.

Isobel found herself revelling in the weightlessness of it. Her soul flew as a feather on a breeze, no longer weighed down.

Maybe Liam had been right about trusting. She could start with the people in this room.

****

The next morning, they woke to sunshine, no wind and Mia with more energy than the small house could contain. A beach trip seemed the only logical answer.

Liam took her hand as they crossed the hot sand.

Bel let him. No need to keep walls up or fight her feelings. Now was the time for recovery. Rediscovery. Her broken mirror portrait came to mind and she could feel light blazing through the cracks, transforming...restoring.

Mia toddled ahead in a swimsuit, her body looking tiny with no bulky nappy. The sunlight played through her shiny hair, gleaming bright highlights as she moved. She stopped after a few steps to kick up sand and wave to a surfer waxing his board.

He waved back, his white teeth gleaming against his dark skin.

Liam leaned in close. "She seems fine coming back here."

Bel slowed her breathing. His nearness rattled her. *Calm down, heart.* "Might be a different story at the driftwood." Sounding normal took every scrap of effort.

He squeezed her hand. "We need to do this. Got to be some answers."

Isobel bit the inside of her cheek to stop laughing. He'd mistaken her breathlessness as concern for Mia. Of course, she was concerned for Mia, but not in a way that would caused her to have such trouble breathing.

The dried-up tree hadn't moved since the last time she'd been down here. She'd been to hell and back, but the wood had stayed put. "There it is."

Mia had drifted toward the gentle lapping of cool, emerald waves.

"Mia! This way, love."

Mia looked up at her name and came running. She swerved towards the wood, squealing with glee. Not quite the reaction Isobel was expecting. They came around the other side, the side where Isobel had found her.

Liam led Isobel, her feet suddenly reluctant.

Mia was sitting on the log by the time they came close. Her legs were swinging, too short to reach the sand. They went to sit by her, but she pushed them with a fervent, "No, no!"

How odd. Isobel asked, "Can we sit by you?"

"Uh-huh."

Isobel went to sit to her left but Mia stood up to push her sideways. "No!"

She sat a bit further down earning a smile from the little girl.

Liam frowned. "Can I sit here, Mia?" He gestured to the open spot right next to her."

She looked up at him as if he'd lost his mind. "No! No, Lim."

"Why not?"

She patted the open space, her face lighting up the way it had on the day she'd vanquished Roric. "Jesus."

"Jesus? Is sitting here?"

Mia nodded, beaming at him for finally getting it.

Bel caught Liam's eye over the top of her head. He shrugged, nose wrinkling in puzzlement.

Mia closed her eyes, raising her face to the sun. "Jesus here al'a time."

"Mia, do you remember being here?"

The tiny girl looked around her, shoulders sagging. She nodded. "Mommy swim. Gone." She stared at her hands in her lap.

Sharp pain tore through Isobel. This is what she was worried about.

Mia patted her legs, dimpled grin returning, "Jesus here. Mommy gone. Jesus here."

Wriggling off the branch, she sat on the sand and began burying her legs with handfuls of fine whiteness, pausing now and then to stare at the sea. Raising both hands, palms up, she asked Bel, "Where Mommy?"

Liam shook sand out of his flip-flop. "She's got a point."

Bel ignored him and sank to her knees in the soft sand next to the orphan. She ran her fingers through Mia's hair, wishing she could weave her love into a blanket to wrap around her. "Your mommy is gone, Mia. But I'm here. Liam is here. I love you, Mia."

Mia took in every word, frowning as she sorted through what it all meant and how it affected her world. Her eyes grew distant, and her face lit up at something beyond were Bel was sitting. "Jesus here." With that, she stood up sending sand flying. Slowly and deliberately she wrapped one arm around Bel's neck and held the other out to Liam.

He sank to his knees from where he'd been perched on the driftwood. As soon as he was close enough Mia slipped her arm around his neck too. For that moment, nothing else mattered.

By 11AM, the heat of the sun and her hungry belly told Isobel it was time to go. She was frustrated. She wasn't sure what she'd been expecting, but she'd hoped to come away with more answers. Instead, all they had were more questions. Mia though, had made her so proud. Such a brave little girl.

They walked holding Mia's hands, one on either side. She'd count to three and lift her legs for them to swing her. Three steps, swing. Three steps, swing.

Bel's left shoulder was on fire from the workout.

Liam pointed. "Look! He's caught a wave."

The surfer who'd caught Mia's attention earlier was far out in the sea, riding the water as if it were a horse beneath him. His body swayed and compensated. He stayed upright nearly all the way to the shallows.

Mia watched him, eyes dancing.

Liam got a look on his face that Bel had come to know so well. "Wait here."

He jogged towards the surfer as he came in from the waves. They spoke. Liam nodded, and then the surfer pointed southwest down the coast. Liam shook his hand and ran back.

"He lost a board out here once. It washed up in a cove five miles down. Maybe we should go see what we can find."

She caught his meaning and her hunger dissolved.

Mia had fallen asleep in her car chair by the time Liam pulled to a stop.

"I'll just stay here by her. Are you happy to go alone?" Bel wanted to kiss Mia for being asleep.

"I was going to suggest you two stay put

anyway." The look on Liam's face stated clearly that he saw straight through her excuse. He took a deep breath and chose a narrow path between overgrown bushes.

Bel sat in silence that was not silent. A cacophony of bug noise surrounded her, undergirded by the bass tones of a bullfrog and Mia's gentle snores. Nature's *Symphony in C Sharp*. It made her smile. Tiny wildflowers dotted the grass around where Liam had parked the car. Her fingers itched for a pencil and paper.

Time alone meant time to think. Not too keen on her own company, she tentatively reached heavenwards.

God, I feel like I'm in the eye of a hurricane. It's peaceful here, yet so much is unresolved. You have heard and answered. You were with Mia through it all. Through the worst of it, she was never alone. Here I am crossing a deep chasm, leaving the old behind. Walking to the new. You are the rock beneath each step that I take. If You don't appear underneath each footstep, I will fall. Yet the question remains, why should You be there for me? Can I trust You to take me all the way across?

No one answered but the crickets and the bullfrogs.

Liam came back close to an hour later, drenched in sweat from the effort of breaking through the dense growth. He was pale, grim lines set into his forehead. Climbing into the driver's seat, he shut the door gently so as not to wake Mia.

Bel saw a tremor pass through his hands on the steering wheel. Too scared to ask, she sat, heart beating in her throat.

"I think I found her. Further south to the beach at the end of the access path. I could"—he swallowed, grinding his teeth—"smell...that something wasn't right. I forced my way through a good mile of overgrown trees and bushes. I came out on a rise overlooking the beach." He shut his eyes, opened them again as if what he saw on the back of his eyelids was too much for him. "Brought in by the tide, snagged on low branches. I'm sure it's her. Here, hang onto this. It might be useful." The pendant he put in her hand hadn't taken kindly to the salt water. She held it gingerly, knowing where it had come from.

He reached across Isobel to get his mobile from the glove compartment and dialled Detective Nass.

31

Isobel didn't do surprises well. A week had passed since they'd found the body. Authorities hadn't yet confirmed her identity, but from the state of the corpse they were able to approximate her date of demise—the day Isobel had found Mia. There was little doubt in Isobel's mind that Mia truly was an orphan.

Liam had taken Isobel to the shops for some headache tabs. Throbbing pain had set in at the base of head and reverberated through the inside of her skull.

She massaged her temples with her forefingers as they pulled up outside home.

Mia chatted nonstop. About birds, the scraggy dog down the road—who was, according to Mia, lonely—Jesus, and why crabs pinch.

All Bel's concerns about taking Mia back to the driftwood had proved baseless. The trip had in fact done the opposite. It seemed to have brought closure for Mia, and the little girl had grabbed life with both hands and was running at full, joyful speed.

Isobel rooted in her bag for fickle house keys.

Liam reached past her and unlocked with her spare which he'd attached to his key ring. She frowned at that, but her head was too sore to push the point.

A lounge full of craft club ladies was the last thing she expected. Squealing with excitement, Kez dragged her through to see their hard work. Pink *It's a Girl* balloons bobbed across the ceiling, ribbons trailing down in curly waves. Mia ran in circles, jumping up to try catch them. Lilac-iced cupcakes, brownies with almond flakes, and sausage rolls covered the coffee table. For Mia there was a special party pack, her name in sparkling glitter.

Bel's eyes misted over, the pain in her head unbearable.

The ladies gathered around, taking turns to hug her.

"What is this?" She forced herself to smile.

Savannah rolled her eyes. "Your baby shower, silly!"

Jules was standing behind a chair they had draped with gold fabric. "Here's your throne, queen mother. Come sit."

Bel stepped carefully through a forest of presents gathered around the base of the chair. The ceiling closed in as she sat on soft cushions.

Mischa put a plate of nibbles in her hand. Everything they had done, all the celebratory pink, hammered the truth home.

Mia was not hers. Everything was not resolved. Her heart remained on the chopping block. "I'm sorry, ladies. I can't do this."

****

Isobel checked her watch, shifted to get comfortable on the metal chair in the warden's office. He walked in carrying folders in his arms, looking harassed. Dumping them on his desk, he sighed. "What can I do for you, Miss Carter?"

"Is it possible for me to speak to Roric MacAllister? Aah, sorry. I mean Greg Smethers. I have questions that need answers."

"I'm afraid that won't be possible."

Bel had known that this was not going to be easy. She had scraped together her courage to get this far and didn't intend to be put off at the first no.

"You don't understand. I need to speak with him. I have issues that need resolving, and he is the only one who has the answers." Smethers knew Mia's mother. Only he would know if she had family...if Mia had a family looking for her.

Isobel's appeal did little more than crease his forehead. "It won't be possible as he is no longer here. Released on bail this morning."

The roof seemed to dip as she clung to her chair, fighting through the swimming blackness. She pushed off the chair to force herself onto her feet. Her gut had been right all along. There was no time to waste. She had to get back home, finish packing, and get out of Scottburgh. In the parking lot, she reached out, key in hand, to unlock the car. Anger bubbled to the surface, a pot left too long on the stove, or rather a volcano crumbling to the pressure of hot lava too long in its belly. *Running.* She'd spent her life running.

Mia deserved more. More than a life of looking over her shoulder.

Resolve settled in the pit of Isobel's belly as she turned back to face the warden. "All I need is his address."

If patience were paper, the warden's would be see-through, worn so thin. "Ma'am, I understand how you feel, but I must strongly advise you to stay away." The man was grinding his teeth in an effort to stay patient. "The fact that some overworked judge decided he wasn't a threat or a flight risk doesn't necessarily make him safe."

Isobel could see she was getting nowhere. *There has to be a way.*

Show me, Jesus.

The warden ushered her out of his office without another word. The door slammed shut behind her. A thin sliver of common sense kept her from kicking it.

The sun scooped low in the sky, trailing long shadows through the reception window.

A female officer shuffled papers at the front desk.

Bel halted, studying her for a moment before going close. Her hands moved efficiently, left hand ring finger showing a faint white circle—a trace of where a wedding ring used to be. It was nearly enough to make Bel smile.

"I wonder if you can help me?"

The officer paused, papers suspended between punch and file.

"The man who has just been released on bail, Greg Smethers. I need to know where to find him."

The papers landed in the file. "I can't help you."

"I need answers. Only he can help." The moisture in her eyes was not part of the act. "I thought I loved him, but all he wanted was to kill me and steal my baby. I just want to hear some things from his mouth."

Papers shuffled. Silence.

Bel held her ground. A quick dab at her eyes with the back of her hand.

"I'm not allowed to give you that information." She met Bel's eyes for the first time since the start of the conversation. Hands shuffled through folders on her desk, and she pulled a slim one out and lay it open on the counter top. "Excuse me for a moment." Index finger tapped on the yellow page. "I'll be right back."

Bel took her cue, scanning for the address. There!

She jotted it down on the back of her hand, closed the folder, and left with a heart heavy, as if someone had draped it in liquid lead.

32

Sitting in her car outside Roric's house, Isobel felt the lava inside turn icy, cooling as the sun set in the distance. Bel wasn't sure what she'd been expecting, but it wasn't this: a pristine white double story with a stone path running from gate to front door in a perfect straight line. The window sills were stark white.

Unease sat uncomfortably between her shoulder blades. All the windows she could see were shut up tight.

Isobel couldn't shake the feeling that she was looking at a graveyard. Sick of all the dead in her head and in front of her eyes, Bel breathed deep, trying to rekindle the fury from earlier.

Procrastination.

She checked her phone. Six missed calls. All Liam. He'd left a voicemail, too. She hid her phone in the cubby hole. She had no intention of listening to it, not now. It wouldn't take much to persuade her that this was a bad idea.

The surprise baby shower had driven her here. *What were they thinking?* Mia was not hers, might never be hers. Only Roric knew where Mia had come from, if the little girl might have family somewhere looking for her. Isobel shivered. And only he knew what had happened to the other missing children. And yet here he was, living in his nice house, as if her world wasn't tearing apart.

Roric must have kept some kind of records—some evidence that could be used to find the missing children and Mia's family, if she had any. As much as it would hurt Bel to give her up, maybe there was a grandmother out there, frantic with worry.

Forty-eight minutes later she decided to get moving. She checked her phone and pocketed it. There'd been no sign of life from inside, and she could feel her fear growing with each passing minute. Waiting here in the shade was doing nothing but eroding her resolve.

Bel crept into the yard through a wrought iron pedestrian gate. Lush green lawn ended in curves around beds of rose bushes, branches hanging low, thick with flowers. She sank down next to a hedge of climbing jasmine. The heady scent tickled her nose. She squeezed the bridge between thumb and forefinger, chasing the threatening sneeze. Crossing the yard, she couldn't help feeling conspicuous, as if the whole neighbourhood were watching, whispering foolishness behind their hands. Before her courage failed, she found an open window and peered inside.

For a moment her brain split in two: one half detached, completely calm, and the other a quivering mess spouting gibberish on its knees. She steeled herself and peeped out from the safety of the curtain. A study of sorts. Nothing moved; nothing breathed. Her gaze swept the room for clues. A chrome and glass desk stood off to one side, a laptop cord trailed across it. No laptop. She scanned the books on the shelves: Freud, Karl Marx...

Jesus, please show me.

She longed to run her fingers across the knobbly wood of the bookshelf, pressing anything that seemed out of the ordinary. A secret passage? *Grief, Isobel, this is not a spy movie. Get a grip!*

She crouched down and moved past a sliding door to the next window. She tented her eyes and found herself looking into a bedroom. There was a weirdness laced through this house that Bel couldn't fathom. It was like walking into the pages of a magazine. Perfect. Beautiful. No heart or personality.

Lamplight cast warm shadows across a loosely woven throw, the colour of desert sand, draped over the end of a king-size bed. The duvet cover was a single shade of ochre, pillows breaking the sparse monotony with splashes of jewel colours. She had to admire his taste. Textured paint decked the walls in a fine sheen. The room was elegant, classy. Nothing out of place. Weird.

The cupboard door was ajar, and she could make out the clothes inside. She spotted the shirt she remembered being impressed with on their first date. She'd been such a fool.

Her gaze travelled higher—a row of Bibles lined up along the top shelf. He seemed to be collecting one of each translation. She couldn't imagine him reading a Bible, even less spending money to build a collection. Weird, but not criminal.

She heard a key in the door. Roric was home.

The door swung open down the hall. Footsteps down the passage.

Coming her way.

33

Liam held Mia on his hip and kissed the top of her head.

She ignored him, licking sticky cake crumbs from her fingers.

Around them, the craft club ladies swirled like eddies in a stream, leaving order in their wake. Sadness hung over the room, the kind that carries a twinge of 'we did something wrong.'

Mischa came over with handfuls of colourful present bags. "What should I do with these?"

Liam didn't know how to answer.

Maggie seemed the least affected by the sombre mood. "I have a feeling that she will need them soon." Her smile washed warm over Liam. "Is there space in a closet somewhere? Maybe this one here in the hall?"

Liam shrugged. "Be my guest. If you can find a space, use it."

Mia bobbed up and down in his arms and stuck her hand out. "Pucake? Peez?"

"You want another cupcake?"

Kez came over and held a plate for her to choose. "Here you go, princess." She ran a hand down the back of Mia's silky head. Her eyes caught Liam's. "Where do you think she's gone?"

Liam had been falling over the same question all afternoon. "I don't know."

After two bites, Mia decided she'd had enough

pucake. She dropped the remainder on the carpet, icing landing in an explosion of lilac. She tucked her hands under her chin and fell asleep on Liam's chest.

"Wow! She nods off fast." Kez chuckled.

"It's a real skill, I tell you." His phone rang in his back pocket. Liam held her awkwardly, trying to reach it.

Kez stepped in to take her. "I'll see to her. You answer your call."

He shot her a grateful look and pulled out his phone.

Isobel! Pressing to answer, he held the phone to his face.

"Hey, girl. Are you OK?"

No answer. All he could hear was muffled noise.

"Where are you?"

The line dropped. A breathless minute later a text came through. An address.

"Isobel, are you OK?"

Another text. *Please come. Roric's house.*

Blood drained from his face, pins and needles blazed through his scalp. "She's at Roric's house."

The ladies spun around from their cleaning, shock on their faces.

Jules dropped a glass. It hit the floor and shattered. "Go to her, Liam. We'll look after Mia."

****

Isobel peered through the blinds, hardly daring to breathe.

Roric left the room.

She could hear clattering in another part of the house. She dialled Liam.

Come on. Pick up.

Liam answered. Footsteps. She hung up.

Roric was back. He sipped amber liquid from a glass and set it down in the pool of lamplight on his bedside table, next to a knife just as ugly as the one he'd held against her.

All she could do was pray that Liam didn't phone her back. She muffled the phone between her hands just in case, switched to text and typed as quietly as she could.

Roric had his back to her, studying something in his hand. He reached over, flicked a switch and bright light flooded the room.

Her hairs stood on end as he turned towards the cupboard and reached for the handle. He took down one of the Bibles, blew a thin layer of dust off, and opened it. He reached into his pocket and took out something. Bel craned her neck to see. The object in his hand was silver, no bigger than his palm. He slipped it into the Bible, shut it, and put it back on the shelf.

Goosebumps broke out all over Bel. She had to see inside those Bibles. Roric picked up his glass, took a sip. He turned to walk out as Bel slipped and bumped the siding below the window. She cringed and pulled her head behind the curtain, hoping it was thick enough that he wouldn't be able to make out her silhouette behind it.

Please, Jesus.

"You!"

Isobel shot up.

Roric moved fast. He must have slipped out the house through the sliding door Isobel had passed, and he now stood towering over her.

Before she could run, he grabbed her. Twisting her

arm behind her back, he pushed her toward the door.

Pain exploded in her shoulder. She kicked against the wall trying to push him off balance, but he was too strong.

His other arm clamped around her ribcage. He doubled her over and brought a knee up into her ribs, knocking her wind out. "Go ahead, scream. Nobody will hear you."

Isobel gasped, fighting for breath. Even if it would help, screaming was not an option. Sucking enough air into her lungs was a struggle.

"You just can't get enough of me, can you." There was no humour in his voice, just pure cruelty. He pushed her through the sliding door and forced her, face down, to the carpet. He stretched up for the tie-back, letting the curtain fall closed.

Trapped under his body weight, Isobel fought rising panic. She kicked, squirming to get out from under him, but he was too heavy. A faint trace of ammonia lingered in the soft fibres of the carpet. It made Bel want to throw up. Who cleans their carpets with ammonia?

Her phone fell out her pocket. Roric kicked it away, out of her reach. He bound her hands behind her back, dragged her to her knees. It felt like being in one of those dreams she had of being chased; her insides writhed but her body went lame. Unresponsive.

He strapped her bound hands to the bedpost. The stiff fabric and wood cut into her wrists.

He picked up his drink and swallowed it all. "You know what? I don't want to deal with you right now. Why don't you just relax and think about what a terrible mistake you made coming here today." Roric sneered at her, shaking his head, then he locked the sliding door and pocketed the key. He pointedly picked up the knife from his bedside and bent down to retrieve her phone. Every movement precise and deliberate, driving home that he was in control. He put off the light and drew the bedroom door behind him as he left. The click of the lock made Isobel wince.

Can't let him win.

Isobel pushed her back against the bed. Breathing was easier now, but her legs shook as she tried to get her feet in under her. It took longer than it should have to slide herself up to a stand. The bedpost was square and wide at the bottom, but tapered to a narrow, smooth circular pole toward the top. If she could only hoist herself higher, the tie might be loose enough for her to slip her hands out.

Working her wrists around the corners of the post took off layers of skin, but she ignored the sting and kept moving. A sheen of sweat covered her forehead by the time she was far enough around to get up onto the bed.

Bel tucked her feet in underneath her on the bed, shimmied her back up the bedpost and pushed. She squirmed herself upright and felt the tension ease in her bonds enough for her to slip one hand out. The other slipped out easily. She'd left muddy footprints on the bedding. The bed creaked as she jumped off and she froze.

She was in the dark, in deep trouble.

The sounds of a laughter track suddenly filled the house, some sit-com on TV. Silence. And then, classical music from *Phantom of the Opera*. Roric liked opera?

Silence. Apparently not.

Heavy grunting and gunfire. This time he didn't change channels.

The noise of the TV was working in her favour. There was no sign that Roric had heard.

Straining her ears for any movement outside the bedroom, she eased the cupboard open and reached up for the Bible. Opening the cover, she gasped. Her eyes had adjusted to the dark enough to see a rectangle had been cut out in the middle of the pages. Inside the hole nestled a flash-stick, labelled in tiny printed letters. She held it toward the faint moonlight coming through a gap in the curtains.

Corinne/Dean. It meant nothing to her. She replaced it, stowed the Bible, and pulled down another. Same thing—hollowed out inside, carrying a flash stick. This one made her blood run cold. Saskia/Mia. The name Isobel had been had been pencilled in beneath the two printed ones. Shock zapped through her body. She nearly dropped the Bible. Her hands trembled as she tried to replace the memory stick and put the Bible away

The room door was locked with the key still in the other side. She waited for what sounded like a bomb blast on the TV to use Liam's trick. With a wire hanger from the cupboard and a thin magazine, Bel got the key and unlocked the door. She counted to three, stepped into the dark passage, locked the door behind her, and slipped the key into her pocket.

All she had to do was sneak past Roric and get out. Simple.

Yet the darkness paralyzed her.

Bel sank to the carpet, sliding her back down the wall. She leaned her head on a bookshelf. She was a fool to think she'd ever leave here alive.

A faint glow down the passage caught her eye. It was coming from a lamp in the corner of the lounge.

The light burned through the blackness like a beacon. One lit-up filament, shone through glass, through fabric. The light it gave off cut straight through the blackness of the passage and reached all the way to where she sat in the dark, shaking. It seemed to land in her heart with a splash of hope.

The Light shines in the darkness, and the darkness has not overcome it.

Her mind flipped to the image she'd drawn in art class, her face shattered beyond hope—yet now not pencil on paper, but flesh. Her flesh. From inside her hollow eyes pulsed a dim throb of brilliance, growing in intensity with each pounding heartbeat. Her drawing in Rachelle's art class foreshadowed what she saw alive in her head now: searing brightness arced through the cracks along her cheeks, her forehead. Dazzling radiance blazed from inside her brokenness.

Don't look to Me as some distant God, aloof from your pain and desperation. Driving you from behind, cracking a whip of fear. I am not hidden as some riddle to be unpicked like a ball of tangled twine. A puzzle to be solved before I can reach down and save.

I AM.

I AM alive inside you. I AM hope that keeps your heart beating from one aching contraction to the next, pumping through pain and agony, not quitting until sweet healing comes.

Do not back down. Do not run. Open up and let Me shine out. Nothing more, nothing less.

I AM.

Giddy joy coursed through her veins, bubbling out of her in silent belly-shaking-chuckles. All this time she'd been looking outside, waiting for the clouds to roll back so she could see the sun. Yet, here He was.

The Son. Alive inside her. What a fool she'd been.

She got to her feet, using the bookshelf to help herself up. Her hand brushed a familiar object on the top shelf — Roric's knife. She pushed it backwards, till it fell behind the bookshelf. He wouldn't find it in a hurry now. Her fingers felt further along the wooden surface — her phone! Roric could have smashed it, but he didn't. Mouthing a silent *thank You*, she switched her mobile to silent and typed a quick message to Liam.

34

Liam pulled up outside the address Bel had sent. He'd driven straight here without stopping to think, no time to formulate a careful plan. All he could imagine was Bel in the hands of that monster. Roric would not touch her, much less hurt her. Not while there was still breath in his lungs.

A familiar beep from his phone.

Isobel.

Stay out. Trust me! Bel.

What on earth?

****

She pressed record, slipped the phone into her pocket and got to her feet. Marvelling at the peace coursing through her veins, pumping through her heart, she took a deep breath and stepped up to the archway leading into the lounge. Making sure she was in clear sight, she cleared her throat.

"Hello, Roric."

His eyes bulged and he swung about looking for something. In two heartbeats, he'd regained composure. His eyes still shifted, hunting. For his blade?

Isobel thought of it tucked safely behind the bookshelf. *Keep looking, you're not going to find it.*

Tension danced through his shoulders. He fell

back on smooth. "Isobel. Full of surprises, aren't you? Can I get you something to drink? Brandy?"

Bel shook her head.

"Pity." Glass decanter clinked against crystal as he poured out a third of a cup. Regarding her with thoughtful eyes, he changed his mind, filled the glass, and downed half of it in one swallow. He grimaced. "So you didn't like your accommodation? I thought it was perfect myself. Just no pleasing some people. Maybe we need to consider a more *permanent* solution for you." He inched towards her, a lion admiring its prey.

Bel had expected to feel fear. She shook her head with a smile. *Uncanny.*

Roric must have picked up on something. He stopped and fidgeted, muttering under his breath. He threw back another mouthful from his glass and then looked her straight in the eye. "Why did you come here, Isobel? Has the young lass Mia proved too much of a handful for you? You want me to take her off your hands? Hmm?"

"You dare even think of touching a hair on her head—"

He flung his hands up in mock-surrender. "Touchy, touchy! My question remains."

A flash of red caught her eye. Hanging on the side wall off a row of hooks were half a dozen red silk ties, identical to those Mia had been tied up with. Acid rose in her throat. "I want to know why."

"Why? Why what? Selling kids? Good money. Single moms? Easy to mess with and get rid of. Is it all a result of my own tragic childhood? Was I getting back at society for the rotten life I was dealt? Or maybe I'm just wicked beyond belief. What do you think,

Isobel? Hmm? You seem to be quite the expert."

Each question felt like a slap on her face. Heat flooded her cheeks. This was how she remembered him, yet someone had turned on the floodlight. Roric's confidence that had once buckled her knees was pure arrogance, the charm—nothing other than manipulation. She ignored his questions, coming back at him with one of her own. "You dropped them off at the police station. Why let them go?"

He blinked and she spotted it again—that feeling that she'd been unable to name. Confusion. Roric was thoroughly confused, and he didn't know what to do with himself. His eyes lost focus. "It was the girl."

"Mia?"

"That one. She got to me."

"How?"

He reached up and took a slender length of red fabric between his hands and then stared at her as if measuring how tight he'd have to pull to snap her neck.

"I'm going to level with you, Isobel. The fact that you aren't dead means there is obviously more to you than I thought. I don't know what's up with that kid of yours, though we both know she isn't yours." His teeth gleamed in the half-light.

A chill skittered down her spine. "Tell me about Mia."

He grimaced and hung his head. Even the reminder of whatever had happened unsettled him. "It was after we'd ditched you at the station. I figured you'd all be tied up in knots scouring the country. So I decided the best thing would be to stay put. We got a room in a nearby hotel and settled in to wait until the heat had died down." His eyes were closed as he relived the memory. "I was getting antsy. Hate waiting. I wanted to finish this transaction and be rid of those three. Such a handful. I still remember the moment it hit. Ben had been whining about needing milk for his sister. It was enough to detonate my skull—his constant whining about food. I yelled at him, told him to shut it if he knew what was good for him. That little girl of yours... fearless. She didn't want to know my trouble before then, but at that moment, she slid off the couch and came to me. She wasn't scared of me at all. When I close my eyes, I see her in front of me—those dark eyes so serious. She crawled up next to me, and climbed onto my lap, looking into my eyes for the longest time." His eyes were closed and goose-bumps had raised the hair all down his arms.

He shook his head, bewildered. "She smiled. I glared at her, but she didn't care. She stretched her arms out, took me round the neck, and hugged me. In that moment, it didn't matter what I'd done to her, or that I'd stolen her from you." His eyes pulled into sharp focus. He sneered at her, cutting off the memory. "It made me uncomfortable. I didn't want them around anymore."

Unflinching, she met his gaze. He broke away and started pacing.

Bel decided to push. "How many others have there been?"

He stopped pacing and glared at her—every muscle taut and his fists clenched around folds of red fabric. "I think it is time you leave." He snapped the fabric between his hands and took a step towards her. "How did you find me? What did you hope to accomplish?" Another step closer.

Light throbbed in her belly. She stared at him, shaking her head slowly. *You don't want to do this. Trust me.*

His eyes widened at what he saw. Bel felt unchanged, but she knew by the look on his face that Light and Life were blazing out of her with the same brilliance and intensity that made him run from Mia. Not visible, yet very much so.

He blanched. "Get out!"

She doffed an imaginary hat at him, tucked her toes behind her foot with a semi-curtsey, turned on her heel, and walked out the front door.

****

Liam sat in the car, gnawing on his fingers. He peered through the blackness as if he could conjure up x-ray vision if only he stared hard enough. Fifteen minutes had passed since Bel's cryptic message. The longest fifteen minutes of his life. The battle in him raged fierce: something was wrong. Rescue the girl! Trust her, stay out! *God, what do I do?*

The question brought no answers, just a hint of stillness, of peace. So he stayed put, though his insides raged like wild stallions held captive by mere twigs. He gnashed and tossed, despising the five words that tied his hands.

Sixty more seconds, and I'm going on.

47…46…45…Every man has a limit. He'd just reached his.

He stared at the face of his watch, counting down.

23…22…21…forehead dripping in salty anguish.

7…6…5…

The door flew open. Isobel! Walking. Not running.

Face wet.

She saw him and her face crumpled. Fierce determination kept her walking—he could see it in her eyes. *I will not run.*

Crossing the street now, coming towards him. He flung the car door open and she threw herself in. Into his arms. Sobs rose in crashing waves.

"Bel, what did he do to you?" Panic constricted his heart, his throat.

The girl was crying too much to speak. Shaking. "No. No!"

Fiery anger ignited. "I swear, I'm going to rip his head off—"

"Liam! No." She was laughing now. What?

Her hand on his chest. "It's OK. I'm good." She pulled her phone out of her pocket. "It's all here."

35

Detective Nass leaned forward, his face grim and a gleam of something in his eye. Admiration?

Bel pressed stop on her phone. Roric's voice cut short.

"Are you willing to testify in court?" Nass asked Isobel.

"Absolutely."

"Then this will do." He held out his hand and she put her mobile into it. "You're going to have to do without this for a while." He reached for his phone. "Excuse me, I need to get a team working on this. Bibles in the cupboard, you say?"

Isobel nodded. "Oh, here is the key to the room they're in. I kind of forgot to give it back."

Nass chuckled as if he couldn't believe what he was hearing, "You go on home, folks. I'll be in touch."

Liam tucked Isobel under his arm and they turned towards the door.

"By the way,"—the detective's face remained deadpan—"good work."

She walked to the car as if floating through candy floss clouds. Surreal.

Liam's arm around her shoulders was a fraction too tight. A tightness that shouted out loud all sorts of unspoken words. He pulled her to face him as they got to the car. Holding both her hands, he leaned over her.

"Isobel Carter, if you ever pull a stunt like that

again—"

"I'll do my best not to. Trust me."

He shut his mouth and squeezed out, "Mmm."

Bel laughed. The poor man was so conflicted, but thoroughly determined not to pick a fight. She changed the subject. "Now, all I need to do is figure out how to go about making Mia mine."

"I know exactly what you mean."

Of course! "Liam! With the information they're retrieving—you might be able to find your boy!"

He looked dazed. "Oh…yes. That, too."

She wrinkled her nose at him. "What were you talking about?"

He brushed off her question. "Doesn't matter. You're right. Wow, Bel. Now there's a thought."

36

Isobel brushed Mia's hair. It was smooth and shiny, no tangles. She'd brushed it less than five minutes earlier, but she did it again anyway.

Mia didn't complain, but yawned sleepily and held her arms out to be lifted up. Bel obliged. The little girl perched on Bel's lap, swinging her new-shoed feet. Purple leather strappy sandals with yellow daisies trailing down the top of each foot stopped just short of where the strap slipped between her big toe and the rest. Head to the side, she examined them, watching the flowers move as she pointed and flexed.

Melindi, pale and drawn, sat opposite, hugging herself against the chill from the air conditioner.

"What's bugging you my friend?"

Melindi shrugged. "It worries me that I fell for it. For him. I never thought of myself as gullible." She bit her lip. "What's to stop it happening again?"

Bel thought for a moment, head tilted sideways. A thought blossomed in her mind with such gentleness, she frowned. Could it be this simple? "I think I get it, Melindi. Way back, actually it was the day I first met Roric...strangely." She shook away the memory. "The zipper on my bag broke. It broke because I'd put too many things in it that it just couldn't take the load. But because the zip wasn't working, two things happened. Important things fell out, I nearly lost my purse — and things I didn't want, went in without me noticing." She wrinkled her nose at the memory of the sticky yellowy-white chocolate mess.

Melindi frowned. "And your point is?"

"Your husband cheating on you broke your zip. Your life was opened up to precious things being stolen and devastating things coming in. Things you'd not normally allow near you had easy access."

Melindi's eyes misted over.

"The funny thing is, Jesus doesn't just fix our zips. He becomes the zip."

No words passed between them. They sat in silent camaraderie, both broken, scarred…but saved and safe.

Isobel, a smile playing on her lips, wrapped her arms around the little girl on her lap. The fierceness of the love that Mia brought out in her was befuddling.

"This bench is going to leave marks on my rear."

Melindi grinned, easing herself sideways with a groan. "Same."

Liam came down the passage from the social worker's office. He was smiling. "Bel, you're up next." He held his hand for hers.

Her stomach flip-flopped. Was it what he said, or how good he looked? Her cheeks grew hot.

Mia to the rescue. She slipped off Bel's lap and grabbed him round the knees so tightly that he nearly fell over.

"Lim! Mine's Lim!"

"Come, Mia. Let's go make Mine your Mommy."

"Mine's Mommy. Yes." She flung an approving smile at Bel, chuckled from her belly, and skipped circles around them as they started down the passage.

Isobel hung back. "We're going to be just fine. You and me."

Melindi was rubbing life back into her numb rear. She nodded. "I think you are right, Bel. Now go get your baby!"

Mia ran ahead, singing something about cows and clouds. Down a long, empty passage, she ran. Not stopping, she kept going straight into the room where a panel of social workers waited to interview Isobel.

Isobel stopped for a moment to breathe. She was about to step into the room, but Liam pulled her back.

"You remember the other day you were talking about making Mia yours and I said I could relate?"

Bel nodded, distracted and eager to get on with the interview.

"I wasn't talking about finding my boy." The words slipped from his lips and hung in the air between them, tentatively wrapped in hope.

In the background, Mia was singing for the social workers. Their laughter and applause spurred her on.

"What exactly did you mean, Liam?"

He was tripping over his tongue in the worst way, and Bel tried hard not to laugh.

"What I mean is…if the position of Mia's dad is available, I'd really like to have a shot at it. I mean, I have really grown to love that kid. She sneaked through all my defences, and I think I'd be miserable if I couldn't see her every day."

Bel smiled. A tiny sting of regret barbed her heart.

Liam stopped flapping and held her gaze. "But it goes way deeper than Mia. As much as I can't imagine life without Mia, I don't want to be without you, either. You didn't sneak through my defences. You uprooted them completely. I want you, Bel. I want you to be my Mine."

Mia came skipping round the corner, grabbed a

hand each and pulled, "Come Mines."

One word, so complete.

Mine.

Mia's Mine. Liam's Mine.

And God's Mine.

All those weeks ago she thought she'd found Mia, but in truth, it was she who had been found.

Mine.

Thank you…

for purchasing this Harbourlight title. For other
inspirational stories, please visit our on-line bookstore
at www.pelicanbookgroup.com.

For questions or more information, contact us at
customer@pelicanbookgroup.com.

Harbourlight Books
The Beacon in Christian Fiction™
an imprint of Pelican Ventures Book Group
www.pelicanbookgroup.com

Connect with Us
www.facebook.com/Pelicanbookgroup
www.twitter.com/pelicanbookgrp

To receive news and specials, subscribe to our bulletin
http://pelink.us/bulletin

May God's glory shine through
this inspirational work of fiction.

AMDG

Free Book Offer

We're looking for booklovers like you to partner with us! Join our team of influencers today and receive at least one free eBook per month. Maybe more!

For more information
Visit http://pelicanbookgroup.com/booklovers
or e-mail
booklovers@pelicanbookgroup.com